BUTT SANDWICH & TREE

WITHDRAWN
WESLEY KING

BUTT SANDWICH & TREE

A PAULA WISEMAN BOOK
New York   London   Toronto   Sydney   New Delhi

SIMON & SCHUSTER BOOKS FOR YOUNG READERS
An imprint of Simon & Schuster Children's Publishing Division
1230 Avenue of the Americas, New York, New York 10020

SIMON & SCHUSTER BOOKS FOR YOUNG READERS
and related marks are trademarks of Simon & Schuster, Inc.
For information about special discounts for bulk purchases, please contact
Simon & Schuster Special Sales at 1-866-506-1949 or business@simonandschuster.com.
The Simon & Schuster Speakers Bureau can bring authors to your live event. For more
information or to book an event, contact the Simon & Schuster Speakers Bureau at
1-866-248-3049 or visit our website at www.simonspeakers.com.
Interior design by Krista Vossen
The text for this book was set in Adobe Garamond.
Manufactured in the United States of America
0722 FFG
First Edition
2 4 6 8 10 9 7 5 3 1

Library of Congress Cataloging-in-Publication Data
Names: King, Wesley, author.
Title: Butt Sandwich & Tree / Wesley King.
Other titles: Butt Sandwich and Tree
Description: First edition. | New York : Simon & Schuster Books for Young
Readers, [2022] | "A Paula Wiseman Book." | Audience: Ages 8–12. |
Audience: Grades 4-6. | Summary: Told from alternating perspectives, two very different
brothers, eleven-year-old Green, who is on the autism spectrum, and his athletic older
brother Cedar, search for the basketball coach's stolen ring after Green is accused
of stealing it.
Identifiers: LCCN 2021022491 (print) | LCCN 2021022492 (ebook) |
ISBN 9781665902618 (hardcover) | ISBN 9781665902632 (ebook)
Subjects: CYAC: Brothers—Fiction. | Autism—Fiction. | Lost and found possessions—
Fiction. | Mystery and detective stories. | LCGFT: Novels.
Classification: LCC PZ7.K58922 Bu 2022 (print) | LCC PZ7.K58922 (ebook) | DDC
[Fic]—dc23
LC record available at https://lccn.loc.gov/2021022491
LC ebook record available at https://lccn.loc.gov/2021022492

For my brothers Adam and Eric,
my first readers and the inspiration for this book

PROLOGUE

The thief watched as another teacher left Palmerston public school, then checked the time.

Five thirty-two p.m. And a new text message from Emerson:

Want to hang out later? I just bought like 45 taquitos. Did you know they come in boxes that big?!

Sighing, the thief tucked the phone away.

There were still two vehicles in the parking lot. One was a familiar navy blue pickup truck, but the other was a definite concern. Who else was still in there? A teacher? A janitor? A parent watching the tryouts?

The thief chewed nervously on a fingernail, tasting some lingering salt from the day's lunch, then made a decision. It was now or never.

Moving swiftly to the side door, the thief hopped off the bike and grimaced at the mud seeping onto the walkway. So long, white shoes. The side door was locked, of course, but that was no problem. Not when you had the key.

The thief quickly slipped down the hallway and into the open gym office, leaving muddy footprints on the tiles. Sure enough, the target was sitting unguarded on the desk: a diamond wedding ring on a gold chain.

Shoving the prize into a jeans pocket, the thief scurried outside again and pedaled away, taking a last look back at the school.

I'm sorry about this. But let's be honest . . . you deserved it.

CHAPTER 1

GREEN

Three days earlier...

I still can't believe they went with Asperger.

Think about it. You have a bunch of kids with social issues and you name them after some dude named Hans *Asperger*? None of the other scientists sounded his last name out? Nobody thought, Wait a second . . . Ps kind of sound like Bs and also are we cool with butts?

And get this: Hans Asperger wasn't even the first one to study the whole autism spectrum thing. Mom read that a supersmart Russian lady named Grunya Sukhareva was on the case in the 1920s. I could have been a Grunyan! That would have been so cool.

But no. I'm an Asperger. A born-and-raised butt sandwich.

It gets worse, if you can believe it. My mom's name is Ashley. My dad's name . . . John. Ashley and John Bennett: the two most boring names in the entire history of humankind. And they are actually pretty boring people except for one teeny, tiny exception: the names of their children.

My older brother's name is *Cedar*. My name? *Green*.

Think about the poor doctor. And here is your little baby . . . oops, they must have written down the color of his face when he came out instead. Oh, that's his name? How . . . unique.

Yep. My parents had two moments of madness, and they both turned into birth certificates.

"Green!" Cedar shouts from outside the door. "You ready?"

"Coming!"

P.S. I am in the bathroom, but don't worry, I'm just brushing my teeth.

I think about changing my name all the time. But Mom says I have to be eighteen, so I've still got seven more years before I can legally un-Green myself.

How do you like Gale? It's like the sound the wind makes: Gaaaaaaaaaaaale.

"Green!"

Cedar pokes his head into the bathroom, scowling. My brother is two years older than me, but he looks way older. His chestnut hair is always perfectly gelled into messy spikes and he wears Dockers and a leather jacket like my dad, who is forty-one. So.

He also got his first zit last week, which he is *really* sad about.

Cedar says I look like an eleven-year-old in "all the ways you can." I'm gangly and knobby and my dirty-blond hair droops over my ears and freckled forehead like a mop. It also seems to want to grow into a mullet and apparently that's not cool, so I have to get the back trimmed all the time.

Cedar tells me what's cool. He said I can either have a party in the front *and* the back or no parties at all. I have no idea what that means, but he was passionate.

Truthfully, I ignore ninety-nine percent of his fashion advice, which is why I wear socks and Crocs to school. I think comfort should play a prominent role in our footwear choices.

Cedar deeply despises my Croc-socks.

"C'mon, Green," he says, checking his phone. "We are *not* going to be late today."

Today is kind of a big deal (read: huge), but also not until after class so I'm not sure why punctuality matters. But that reminds me of the insanity I agreed to and now my stomach hurts.

"I don't think I can do it," I gurgle through some green spearmint toothpaste.

Peppermint makes me sneeze. Honestly. One piece of peppermint gum and *achoo!* So does the glare of the sun. Once I had peppermint gum on a sunny day and I swear I almost died.

Cedar frowns. "You're almost done now, just spit it out—"

"No," I cut in, though I do spit out the toothpaste. "The . . . you know."

"Oh." He claps my right shoulder. Cedar does that, like, forty-five times a day. Dad told me it's what guys do instead of hugging, but I don't see the correlation. "Just play it by ear. I told you: No pressure whatsoever."

Cedar says that after several weeks of intense daily pressuring, of course. Then he checks his hair—he always finds at least one spike that needs adjusting, though I can never tell the difference—and starts for the stairs.

"Cedar?" I call after him.

"What?"

"Do you think I should gel my hair today?"

Cedar smiles. "Nah. Go au naturale, little bro. It's your style."

"Right."

I look in the mirror and take a deep breath. My dad is excited. My mom is freaked out. I am freaked-out-excited. I don't like change as a general rule. But I already agreed, and Cedar is, like, *extra* excited, and really, how bad can it be? Cedar plays basketball and he's as happy as a clam.

I wonder if clams are actually happy. I guess they get to relax a lot but people also eat them, so . . .

"Green!"

"Yeah! Coming."

I hurry downstairs and get my Crocs on. It takes three seconds because no laces.

Cedar just shakes his head.

"Do you like your name?" I ask him.

I ask him this question every few months to see if he's changed his mind. We have a bit of a routine.

"Could be worse," he says, as always.

"Like what?"

"Birch. Crabapple. California Redwood. Never mind the Butt Plant."

I laugh as he locks the front door behind us. Mom and Dad both work really early, so we get ready for school ourselves. We usually come home to an empty house, too, so I guess we're officially latchkey kids.

I zip my jacket right to the top. It's late September in the suburbs of Toronto, and it's starting to feel cool in the mornings.

"Is Butt Plant a thing?" I ask skeptically.

"It's a thing. It actually looks like a butt. And I like Green, too, by the way."

I shake my head. "It's literally the color of vomit."

"It's perfect! Cedar and Green. We could have been Pine and Pink, man. Or Butt Plant and Blue! *That* would have been rough. We are lucky. We're like a coniferous superteam."

"Lucky?" I ask. "We're already Butt Sandwich and Tree."

Cedar snorts. "For the last time, only you refer to yourself as Butt Sandwich."

"For now," I say darkly, then kick through a pile of fallen leaves on the sidewalk. "What if I suck today, Cedar?"

"You won't," Cedar says, slinging his arm around my shoulders. "Trust me, bro. It's going to be a good day."

"Green?"

"Yes?" I say quietly.

It's my not-in-my-own-house voice. I also have a not-in-my-own-house brain. It's like, Oh, I am in my room with Cedar so I can tell a joke and laugh at stuff. But then I am in the classroom with not-Cedar so I'll just stare straight ahead and not tell jokes because maybe other people don't like . . . stuff.

Yeah. It doesn't make a lot of sense.

P.S. If you don't know much about Asperger's syndrome, don't worry. Neither do I. It's super confusing. Even our family doctor, Dr. Lee, couldn't figure it out at first. He sent me to a bunch of child psychiatrists when I was younger. It was autism for a while and then, "Maybe he's just shy," but, "Hmm, why does he eat the same sandwich every day and not speak to anyone?" and then, "Wait . . . he's one of those unfortunately named Asperger kids!"

And then lo and behold: Everything made sense.

Everything became a *symptom*.

Okay. So I still eat the same sandwich. But hear me out: White bread, a light smear of mayonnaise, and a single slice of processed cheddar cheese is the peak of food. No random spices in there waiting to attack my stomach.

Like star anise. It legitimately looks like poison.

And sure, I didn't talk until I was six. But what was I going to talk about? Politics? The meaning of life?

Dr. Lee always mentions my "rigid routines" too. But I just do the things I like. Now you want me to hit the randomizer button every three days? And today we get: star anise sandwiches, rubber boots, and class socialite.

Even if I survived the spices . . . can you imagine the foot sweat? No thanks.

Mom is always like, "It's no big deal, Green . . . you just have a neurological disorder." But here's the thing: I'm actually *more* ordered than most people, so shouldn't I have a neurological superorder? Congratulations, Mr. and Mrs. Bennett: Your son has a superorder! You better go buy some mayo.

Oh, I also roll a bouncy ball around my left palm when I get nervous, but bouncy balls are awesome so I'm good with that one.

There are a couple of things I would change, I guess. I have a hard time talking to other people, even teachers, which makes school tough sometimes. Not the actual schoolwork; I just have a hard time taking direction or participating in class. Making friends is a no-go. I also space out a lot. Like . . . once or twice in an hour.

All together it's enough that Mom still wanted me to go see an actual Asperger's syndrome specialist, and Dr. Lee finally referred me to Dr. Shondez. She's one of the leading experts in the world on Asperger's syndrome, and Mom had to book my appointment, like, a year in advance.

It's less than two weeks away now, and I am *super* nervous.

Dr. Lee has been suggesting to my parents for a while that I take medication to help me focus, but Mom and Dad weren't sure that was necessary, and I didn't really want to take it either. He also said I might benefit from a private school with smaller classes . . . which would mean going to a different school than Cedar, who would never agree to leave his beloved Palmerston Panthers. Even if he wanted to, Mom and Dad told me they couldn't afford two private school tuitions.

Mom, Dad, and I actually visited a private school called Trafalgar a couple of months ago—without telling Cedar. It was really nice and all, but after the tour, I told them I wanted to stay at Palmerston with Cedar. They said it was my call . . . with one condition: If Dr. Shondez thought some changes would be good for me, they wanted to "revisit" the discussion. Including the medications.

I really don't want to take pills. I'm happy with myself, even if no one else seems to be.

Oh shoot. Mrs. Strachan is looking at me.

Well, *down* at me. She looms. She's really tall, with bright red hair like a campfire, and she smells like maple syrup for some reason. Maybe she eats pancakes every morning. If I was going to go wild one day and eat something else, it would totally be pancakes. They're the plain cheese sandwich of breakfast.

Still looking. What do I do?

This is when my old teacher's assistant would whisper some sage advice like, "Remember when I told you too much yawning can be offensive?" But I'm in sixth grade now and I don't have a TA anymore . . . either because I am "functional" or because there were budget cuts. Mom thinks it was the second one.

Last year the school decided I didn't need an Individualized Education Plan anymore, either, because I was testing so high. Even my TA said I was ready to fully reintegrate into classes without her. That all sounded like good news to me, and Dad agreed, but Mom was worried it was too soon.

She liked when I had a TA, but I think she also pictured a secret agent with glasses on who would billy club kids who teased me.

Here's the thing: Most kids don't really tease me. They just kind of move *around* me. I guess for one I'm pretty tall, and two I don't talk much (like a ninja) so it just makes sense to avoid me.

There are exceptions, of course. Like, S'up, dude, where's your bro at? Or, What's your last name, Bay Packers?

I still have no idea what Carl Freburg was talking about, but he thought it was super funny. And then there's the dreaded Allison Gaisson, of course. She sits right behind me and says something mean, like, every five minutes. Whoever makes the annual class lists clearly has a personal vendetta against me, because we've been in the same math class two years in a row.

"Are you feeling all right, Green?" Mrs. Strachan asks from, like, nine stories up.

Finally . . . a hint! I try to make the connection. We're doing math and I do have my math book open so that checks out. Am I drooling? No, my mouth is dry. Shoot . . . I probably shouldn't have poked it like that. *What does she mean*? I'm wearing pants. They're even khakis . . . it's my fancy day.

Why can't she be specific? I like specifics. Green, why are you frothing at the mouth?

". . . Yes . . . ," I say, because I am truly stumped.

I slip the bouncy ball out of my pocket and roll it around in my left palm.

"You were staring out the window for the last twenty minutes."

Ohhhhh. That makes sense. I did see three V formations of migrating geese.

"Sorry."

"Are you bored?" she asks.

"Yes."

Oh, by the way . . . I *stink* at lying. Cedar says it's my kryptonite.

Mrs. Strachan clears her throat. I do know what that means. It means she would yell at someone else, but this is Green the special quiet boy so she'll just yell inside her throat instead.

"Well, we do have homework for later, and I need to make sure you understand it—"

"I already did mine."

She frowns. "We're doing the questions on page seventy-seven as well."

"I did those too to be safe. I have practice tonight, so I wanted to plan ahead."

Mrs. Strachan stares at me for a moment. Her equally campfire-colored eyebrows are almost touching. If I had to guess, I would say she is either confused or has a migraine. "For . . . "

"Basketball."

Now the other kids are looking at me too. I can hear Allison muttering something behind me. I can't make it out, but I'm sure it's insulting. Lyesha is mouthing "Basketball?" to Mel.

I squeeze the bouncy ball even tighter.

"You're . . . on the basketball team?" Mrs. Strachan says, as if struggling to find the words.

"Well, no. It's a . . . tryout."

Klieba Zanowski sits to my immediate right, and he gives me a strange look too. But he doesn't talk to anybody either, so he just goes back to his math work. I like Klieba.

Mrs. Strachan smiles and blinks a lot. It's like she might . . . cry? "Good for you, Green."

Then she taps my desk with her index finger and almost skips back to the whiteboard. I didn't even get in trouble. So . . . I guess I can stare at geese again because I might go bounce a big orange ball later? No. I get it.

It's me. Green the Butt Sandwich is going to try to play sports like a real boy.

It's all because of Cedar. He's the star player, and I'm pretty tall too, so Coach Nelson asked me to come try out for the varsity team . . . even though I'm only in sixth grade and should technically be trying out with the JVs. And even though I have never played organized basketball *period*.

I'm about ninety-nine-point-nine percent sure it's because Cedar begged him to do it, but Coach really did seem sincere last week. He claimed it would be good for me. "Sports build social skills, son."

I don't know if that's true, but hey, I can bounce things. Cedar and I throw bouncy balls around on my driveway all the time. We have this game where we throw a ball straight up in the air and try to catch it on the first bounce. My driveway is all cracked and bumpy, so it's way harder than it sounds.

It's another reason I always keep one in my pocket . . . for emergency bouncing opportunities. Like if we suddenly got access to an airport tarmac or a mall parking lot or something. Can you imagine the bounces?

But nobody else likes rubber balls apparently, so I have basketball sneakers in my backpack.

Lyesha turns in her chair and leans toward me. "That's so cool, Green."

I manage to smile even though my cheeks are possibly on fire. Lyesha is not in my talking circle . . . and yet she just talked to me. And she was really nice. Maybe basketball *is* good for social skills.

I try to imagine some weird future where I'm like Cedar. I can almost hear the announcer: Starting at, you know, one of the positions, Green Thomas Bennett, the star of the Palmerston Panthers, whose name will eventually be Gale, so everyone shout, Gaaaaaaaaaaaale.

It seems stressful, but I really do like the sound of that name.

Maybe this will be a good day.

CHAPTER 2

CEDAR

"One more try, Fro-Mo," I say, hurrying back into position with my basketball.

It's the last break of the day, and I should be using this time to prep Green for his potentially life-altering first-ever tryout, but I feel like I am *so* close. This could be the big one.

The viral video that shoots me into superstardom.

"Dude—" Mo protests.

"Last time," I cut in, already bouncing on my toes. "I promise. I got this one."

Mo sighs and gets the phone ready. "Take . . . eighty-nine? Action."

I burst into motion, dribbling the ball twice through my legs before spinning around and shooting a three-pointer *backward* over my right shoulder. I wait a seemingly endless second for the usual disheartening clank off the rim. Instead, I hear the sweetest sound on earth: *swish.*

Holy meatballs . . . I made the shot.

Okay, play it cool, Cedar. Just strut into the metaphorical sunset like this always happens and . . . perfect.

I can almost hear the pinging of their hearts.

"Yeahhhh, boy!" Mo shouts, running over for a chest bump.

We huddle together to watch the video on my phone and yeah . . . it's pretty baller. I probably should have done a fake drive first, but regardless, this is *definitely* the big one.

"Tree," Mo whispers, "it's awesome."

I notice that nobody else is cheering or anything and realize the rest of the guys are kicking a soccer ball around out in the field. We were playing basketball, like every other recess, but then Mo tried a backward shot and we looked at each other and were like, Yeah we're filming a video *right now*.

So it took a little while. Whatever.

I do my routine check on Green and spot him sitting in his usual spot next to the first portable classroom. He has an enormous book splayed out in front of him . . . probably one of those crime thrillers he shares with Mom. Green reads a huge book like that every week. He is *ridiculously* smart.

Just past the row of faded white portable classrooms looms Anderson High School, less than a hundred yards away from Palmerston. It's bigger and newer and is always surrounded by high school kids wandering around (when do they go to class?!). More importantly, the singular Keesha Adams attends that school.

I scan the area for her as always, but no such luck.

Keesha hangs out with Coach's daughter, Abby, which is how I first saw her. Abby came to one of our games last year and brought Keesha with her. It was love at first sight. For me. Not sure Keesha looked up from her phone.

We would be so perfect together.

"Think this one could actually go viral?" Mo asks in a hushed voice.

"Absolutely. I need a cool caption, though. And a song when the ball goes in."

Mo strokes his chin thoughtfully. He actually has a few curly black hairs on his chin and upper lip, which is super impressive at thirteen. Mo is short for Mohamed, and he's been my best friend since second grade when his family moved here from Somalia. Mo is the second best player on the basketball team with the best hair by far . . . he has a humungous Afro.

"What about 'Sicko Mode' for the caption?" Mo says. "And then when the shot goes in the actual 'Sicko Mode' beat drops—"

"We did that three times already!" I protest, trying some different filters.

Mo hesitates. "I know, but hardly anyone saw them. You've only got nine hundred and eight followers—"

"Nine hundred and eleven," I mutter, double-checking the number. Mo only has two hundred and one, so we decided to focus on my account for our "premier content" since I had the higher starting count. But it's moving at a trickle. Ten new followers in the *last month*. "We just need a hit."

"Maybe we should try *one* dance routine—" Mo says.

"No," I cut in, scowling. We've had this argument a thousand times already, so it's a sensitive subject. "We do trick shots, man. We're ballers."

"Fine," he mutters. "Why is Green talking to those girls?"

I jerk my head up and see two sixth graders blocking Green from view. "Hey!"

Running over, I recognize Mel and Lyesha from his class and feel my temp rising. People are pretty good with Green. I mean, they should be: Green is awesome. But once in a while some-body makes a stupid comment and last year I got in a fight with Carl Freburg and—

"What are you doing?" I demand.

Green is bright red and trying very hard to read his book.

Lyesha frowns. "We were just asking him about his tryout later. It's so cool."

Okay, I wasn't expecting that. But I see Green's left hand squeezing that bouncy ball he always has on him, and that's one of his tells. I bought him an actual stress ball once with my allowance, but he said it was more about "the potential of bouncing" than the squeezing.

I don't get it, but Green does lots of things I don't understand.

"Well, we're not sure about that yet," I say, forcing a smile. I really need to stop reflexively yelling at people. "But, you know . . . thanks. Can I talk to Green alone for a second?"

Lyesha shrugs. "Sure. Good luck tonight, Green!"

I'm trying to figure out if she's being sarcastic or not, but if she is, she's a total pro.

"You cool?" I ask, looking Green over as the girls walk away.

He nods. His eyes are big and pale, like washed-out blue jeans, and they are always moving . . . mostly to avoid meeting anyone's gaze. His hair is getting too long at the back again.

Honestly, I need to start keeping some clippers in my pocket. If he's rocking a mullet *and* Croc-socks, his social life is going to be over before it can even begin.

"They were just being nice," Green says, slipping the bouncy ball back into his pocket.

"No doubt," I say. "You're a born lady-killer."

"Don't start."

"You know green is the actual color of love? Dad said it either was Green or Casanova."

Dad and I have this ongoing thing where we find out cool facts about the color green, since my brother is so anti-his-own-name. We've used up every Incredible Hulk reference, unfortunately.

The Green Goblin did not go over well. That was Dad. He's a dingbat sometimes.

Green cracks a smile and buries his head in his book. "I am currently occupied."

"Fine. But I need a cool caption for a backward-shimmy-one-handed-shot video. Go."

Green pauses. "No idea what you just said, but how about, 'When you just can't miss.'"

"Boom!" I say. "You're like the Rick Riordan of the caption world."

"Lucky me," Green says, still staring down at his book. "Mo is waiting."

I glance over my shoulder. Mo is standing right where I left him, scrolling through his phone and ignoring us. It's the one great flaw in our friendship—Mo doesn't like being around Green.

I tell him all the time that Green is cool . . . but Mo always gets awkward around him and sometimes just flat-out avoids Green now. Basketball is going to fix that problem, too. I know it.

Everyone is finally going to see the same Green I do.

"You're still coming to the tryout tonight, right?" I ask.

Green's left hand slides toward the bouncy ball again. But he nods. "Yeah."

"My man," I say, then run back over to Mo. "I got the caption! This is it!"

We huddle together and upload the video to TikTok. And yeah, I use "Sicko Mode" for the beat drop, but it really is perfect for that baller sunset-walk-off.

Mo and I grin at each other as I hit the post button. And then we wait.

One heart. Two!

"It's poppin' already!" Mo says.

The bell goes, and I have to tuck the phone away as we line up and head inside . . . but not before I see another heart.

It's totally happening. This is it.

"It wasn't it," Mo whispers from the desk beside me.

"It's only been two hours!"

But I hear the desperation in my voice. I still have nine hearts. *Nine.* There is an algorithm. If you don't start strong, you are in trouble. There are no comebacks on TikTok.

"I still liked 'Sicko Mode' as a caption," Mo says.

I rub my forehead in exasperation. What do I have to do?!

This is my forty-first video. I have the content. Full-court shots and that one where Mo tried to dunk and landed flat on his back instead . . . that was gold!

"Think we can get back on the roof of the school?" I ask, chewing on my bottom lip.

It had been an ambitious attempt the very first week of school . . . and we got caught in the act by Principal Nickel. There was a lot of yelling.

"Nickel did say next time was a one-week suspension," Mo says. "My mom almost killed me."

"Yeah . . . same."

His mom is almost as strict as mine. But Mo got a double whammy because his dad is strict too and mine is super chill. Dad takes me to most of our tournaments and just gives me money and is like, "Come back eventually, dude." Then he gives me props and he goes to the hotel gym.

My dad is *jacked*. He's like half man, half biceps and probably the buffest software engineer on earth. The only downside is he really likes to show it off.

He wears a lot of Spandex.

"Cedar Bennett," a loud voice says, "what did I tell you about that phone?"

I sigh and tuck it back in my pocket. "My social media life is not as important as my grades," I recite.

Mrs. Clark nods. "Exactly. I know everyone just wants to Tik Book these days."

"Wow," Mo says.

"But having phones in class is a privilege," she continues.

"One I don't understand and vehemently disagree with—you should have seen the last PTA meeting—but I *can* retract it."

Mrs. Clark is super old. Wrinkles crease her ebony skin, and she has a shock of short, pure white hair. I would say she's in her seventies, but Mo says she would be retired by then. So . . . sixties? How long can you teach? She's really nice and is probably the best math teacher I've ever had, but she is not a fan of technology.

I put on my most apologetic smile. It makes my cheeks hurt. "Sorry, Mrs. Clark."

"All right," she mutters. "But pay attention. Math is not your strong suit. Well it is, but that's because Green does all your homework."

Mo starts laughing into his hands, and I shoot him a look.

"I always do my own homework, Mrs. Clark," I say, which is kind of true because I'm the one who actually *writes* the answers. Green just tells them to me sometimes.

Okay. All the time.

I'm pretty good in most of my classes: English and history are always straight As (along with gym, obviously), and I get solid Bs in almost everything else. But for some reason my brain is not into math. It sees numbers and just peaces out all of a sudden.

Thank goodness I have Green for a brother.

"Sure you do," Mrs. Clark says, rolling her eyes.

She goes back to the whiteboard, finishing an equation that I do not even remotely understand.

Meghan Hayes glances back at me, smiling and brushing her

hair behind her ear. She does that a lot. Cherene said Meghan has a "massive crush" on me, which is nice and all, but my heart is already dedicated to the aforementioned and completely unattainable Keesha Adams.

Why is she unattainable?

Well, for starters, Keesha Adams is not only in high school, she's in *tenth grade*. I know . . . I've lost my mind. Even Mo says so. Fifteen-year-olds don't date thirteen-year-olds. It's probably never happened in the entire history of the world. Or at the very least at Palmerston public school. I don't think Keesha even knows my name—and she never will at this rate.

I check my TikTok again.

"Still only nine likes! Honestly, I shot it *backward*, people."

"Next time," Mo whispers. "Day's almost over, bro. Time to play some ball."

"Yeah," I say, checking the dusty old clock that hangs above the door. That thing stops during math class, I swear. "I hope Green does well today."

Mo shakes his head. "I still don't think this a good idea, Tree."

Neither does my mom. She's made that *very* clear.

I feel a surge of frustration. "He's going to be good down low, dude. He's tall—"

"Cedar!"

"Sorry, Mrs. Clark."

But Mo's in my head now. I watch the clock possibly ticking and wonder if maybe this wasn't the best idea after all. Did I push Green into the tryout? What if he gets upset? What if someone says something mean and I have to punch them in the head? I really will get suspended.

The bell goes, like, ten days later, and I take a deep breath. It's time for Green's big tryout.

And I don't just mean for basketball.

Chapter 3

GREEN

The thing about laces is they are a tripping hazard. It's one of many reasons why I love Croc-socks . . . they won't just go all loosey-goosey one day and trip me down a flight of stairs.

But Cedar insists I need sneakers for basketball, so I make sure I triple knot them before I step on the court. Whatever else goes wrong in this tryout, it will *not* be laces.

I look up from my spot on the hard wooden bench—why are there no cushions?—and my stomach is feeling just as knotted as my laces. All the other boys are gathered in the middle of the gym, talking and laughing while Coach Nelson puts out some bright orange cones.

Coach sees me watching and shoots me a thumbs-up, so he either appreciates footwear prudence or is just happy I came.

To be honest, I can't believe I am there either.

I brainstormed a bunch of excuses on the walk down the hallway. I was thinking appendicitis, but it felt a bit dramatic.

And hey . . . I can do sports. It's not my first rodeo. You know when you're five years old and you play soccer, but really you just run around in a swarm and some kids pick daisies? I was definitely picking daisies. Apparently I once chased a butterfly four soccer fields over and then rejoined the wrong game for, like, twenty minutes until my mom found me. She yelled at the coach, and he wisely advised her that I might not be cut out for soccer. I never went back.

Wait . . . maybe I can't do sports. Oh well. Too late now.

Cedar is standing in the middle of the group of boys. He's a head taller than everyone else so it's pretty easy to spot him—it's partly why he got the nickname *Tree* from his teammates . . . the other reason should be obvious—and he's also the star player, so the group forms around him like planets in a solar system.

Taking a last shaky breath, I shuffle over to join the others, making sure to check my laces one last time for any signs of treachery. I wonder if they make basketball Crocs.

"What's up, bro?" Cedar says, hurrying over and clapping my left shoulder. Honestly, it's amazing I don't have a constant bruise on that shoulder. "You ready?"

I nod. The other boys are all looking at me. Most look confused.

I've done a lot of work learning how to recognize emotions in faces—Mom used to print out these special activity sheets—and I always thought *confused* was one of the easiest ones to identify . . . the deep frown lines usually give it away.

I like frown lines. Our mouths are better at smiling, but our eyebrows were born to be confused.

Some of the other faces are trickier. I think Corrado is . . . skeptical? Maybe constipated. A ton of faces look constipated, when you think about it. Mo is rolling his eyes, so that's . . . disdain? Carl Freburg is staring at me like I have something on my face, but I just went to the bathroom and didn't notice anything in the mirror. It seems unlikely anything has changed since then—

"So, the drill is easy," Cedar says, taking my shoulders and repositioning me to look out over the scattered cones. "We just dribble through the pylons and lay it up for ten minutes. Coach might shout out to shoot from the elbow or something instead, so just listen up."

"How do you shoot from the elbow?" I whisper.

Cedar glances at me, frowning. "It's the corner of the key."

"There's a *key*?" I ask, truly puzzled now. "Is there a lock, too?"

"What? No. The paint." He sighs and points beneath the hoop. "The blue area."

"Gotcha."

"We should have done some YouTubing," Cedar murmurs. "Remind me later."

Coach Nelson lays the last cone down and stalks back to the group. He's fairly short for a grown-up, with pale white skin and permanently red cheeks, and he blinks about half as much as a regular human being. He is almost always wearing sweatpants and a really tight T-shirt that exposes tufts of curly black neck hair.

Coach is kind of famous at Palmerston public school for two very different reasons. The first is that he is extremely loud. It's like someone strapped an invisible loudspeaker to his face, and he should know that, but he shouts anyway.

The second reason is that he *always* wears a gold chain with a diamond wedding ring on the end.

It was his wife's ring, but she died two years ago, and now Coach never takes it off. Like . . . ever. The rumor is he even wears it in the shower.

I do a double take. He isn't wearing the ring.

"Did Coach lose his ring?" I whisper to Cedar.

Cedar snorts. "Yeah, right. Coach just takes it off for ball now." He lowers his voice. "Last year he broke the chain at an away game—there was a lot of hand flailing that day—and he almost lost the ring, so he said he better make an exception for basketball. Mo was like, 'Maybe you should try meditating, Coach,' and then we all had to run wind sprints for twenty minutes."

"I see," I murmur.

Coach's unblinking eyes pass over the group . . . and then land on me. He's like half man, half lizard. Except with a ton of neck hair. Wait . . . *will that happen to my neck eventually?*

I look away, rubbing the soft skin back there. I guess it would be nice in the winter. . . .

"Welcome to tryouts," Coach booms. "I'm looking forward to another great year."

"We didn't even make the playoffs last year, Coach," Mo says.

Coach pauses. "No, but we were close. And we have new blood this year."

Some people look at me, including Carl Freburg. There's that mysterious stare again. What does it mean? I check my teeth with my thumbnail. Maybe there is a piece of cheese stuck in there? Unlikely, though . . . on top of being delicious, cheese sandwiches are basically impervious to teeth-sticking.

"We're going all the way this year, right, Tree?" Corrado says, giving my brother props.

"You know it, bruh," Cedar replies.

Ugh . . . do I have to talk like that if I make the team?

"I don't want anyone getting complacent," Coach says, waving a stubby finger at the group. "Just because you were on the team last year doesn't mean you're guaranteed a spot."

Clearly this is meant to be an intimidation speech, but Cedar is smiling because *he* is guaranteed a spot. I watched two games last year and Cedar was the best player by far.

I'm not smiling, because I suck.

"I'll post cuts after each tryout," Coach continues. "After the second one we will have a team. Got it?"

"Yes, Coach!" everyone shouts but me.

How did they know? Is there a secret code in his hand movements?

"Layup line," he says, drawing circles in the air for some reason and then clapping. Maybe there is a secret code . . . I'll have to ask Cedar later. "Let's have a good one, boys!"

All of a sudden kids are running and grabbing basketballs and there is a *lot* of squeaking. It's like a cave full of bats. I have no idea what's happening, so I just fall in line behind Cedar.

I analyze the setup for a moment. It seems simple enough: dribble the ball through some zigzagging orange cones, lay up for a . . . score or whatever it's called, and then join the other line and do it again.

Mathematically speaking, I'm not sure how Coach intends

to account for varying player speeds and skill levels to maintain two even lines, but maybe it's just kind of informal.

I bounce anxiously on my toes . . . after a quick check of the laces, of course.

Okay, Green. You can do this. You just practiced dribbling with Cedar last night. And yes, the ball hit your foot and went into the road and almost got run over by Mr. Benny's pickup truck, who yelled at us but—

"Ball!"

Someone shouts the warning just as an orange meteorite heads for my face. I barely manage to catch it. That could have hit me in the nose! There is a disturbing lack of safety awareness going on around here. Is there a first aid kit available? Tourniquets? A *bag of ice*?

But the drill seems to have begun, so I start dribbling through the cones with one hand way out in front of me to keep the ball away from my foot. I take my time, get to the hoop . . . and hit the underside of the rim.

Hmm. Clearly I'm standing too close. What if I back up a little—

"Move!" someone shouts.

Andrew Staff comes flying in for a layup and almost slams into my spine. Okay, this is *not* like basketball in the driveway. Cedar and I take turns shooting and there is no reckless charging at each other's vertebrae.

Shaking my head in disapproval, I pass the ball ahead and join the next line, which is already longer than the first one.

I knew it. We're going to have one long line soon.

"I'm just saying . . . the PS5 is mad expensive," Carl Freburg is saying ahead of me.

I perk up at the mention of a topic I actually enjoy.

"I know, man," Corrado says from in front of him. "My parents gave me a hard no."

Carl shakes his head. "I *need* some coin, bruh. But where am I gonna get four bills?"

Ahead of us, Cedar darts through the pylons, fakes a behind-the-back pass, and easily lays up the ball. Some of the guys whoop and shout, "Get it, Tree!" I make a few mental notes on his form: two steps, left-foot takeoff, be more athletic . . .

I start again. And I really, really suck.

Okay, I make three layups out of nine, which seems reasonable, but no one else seems to miss that many. My "elbow" jumpers are worse: I make one of seven. And *zero* three-pointers. Obviously. Why would I want to shoot from that far away? I also accidentally kick the ball into the corner at one point, but thankfully Mr. Benny isn't driving his pickup truck around in here.

I can tell I'm doing badly because some of the boys laugh when I miss. Carl shouts that I couldn't hit the side of a barn—not sure how that's relevant—and Mo buries his face in his hands after I airball my third straight shot.

Basketball *looks* simple enough, but my body has always been a little . . . off. It's like someone assembled me and forgot a couple of screws at my shoulders and knees but it was lunchtime and they were like, Close enough, let's leave this butt sandwich and grab a panini.

30

We get a water break, and then Coach tells us we are going to go right into a scrimmage, since "we have so many players." I think he means, So I can start cutting people.

"How's it going so far?" Cedar asks, plunking down on the bench and mopping his sweaty forehead with an equally sweaty sleeve. It doesn't accomplish much.

I was mostly walking so I just have sweaty armpits.

"I stink," I mutter. "I mean at basketball. But also maybe in general."

He laughs. "You just need to keep working, bro."

"I guess."

He claps me on the shoulder and pulls me up. "I can't wait to play together this year!"

Cedar runs back onto the court again, whooping and clapping his hands excitedly. I shuffle after him, holding back a sigh. He's going to be super disappointed when I get cut.

Coach blasts his whistle—I swear even his whistle is louder than normal—and the scrimmage begins. So does the yelling. I knew Coach screamed a lot but, like, he never stops. It's just a constant stream of "Screen!" "Drive!" "Shoot!" and other various one-word directions, except also, "Green, are you paying attention!?"

"Not really," I say.

Coach frowns.

"Green . . . get to the post!" Cedar shouts, jerking his chin toward the hoop.

Right. Carl is alone down there, and I'm pretty sure I'm supposed to be covering him.

I hurry over and stand beside Carl for moral support or something. No, wait . . . the opposite of that. Should I say something vaguely pessimistic? That doesn't seem nice and also Carl is kind of scary. Hmm. I look around for guidance.

"You're going down, Green," Carl mutters.

That sounds ominous. Carl is *big*. He's an inch or two shorter than me, but he's burly and strong, with legs thicker than my waist. He always wears a ball cap at recess, and his shaggy, sandy-brown hair has these little wings at the bottom when he takes it off, like he's wearing a domed helmet. Most notably, he's missing one of his teeth.

Cedar told me he "lost it during a hockey practice." What does that even mean?!

I take a cautious step back, but Cedar shouts, "Stay close to him, Green!" which is unfortunate because of the threats and also because Carl smells like malt vinegar.

I know the smell because Opa eats a ton of fish and chips. Opa is truly baffled by my plain cheese sandwiches. Every time I see him it's like, What about a juicy pear? A nice steak? Can I at least put havarti cheese on your sandwich?

No, Opa. Cheddar or death.

"Ball!" Carl calls, lifting his hand.

Please don't pass him the ball, please don't pass him—

The ball sails over to him. Great. Now I have a real dilemma. I put my arms up because I hear Coach shouting that instruction, but Carl keeps backing up, pushing me toward the hoop. He almost steps on my feet, like, *three times*. If my shoelaces weren't triple knotted, I would be in serious peril.

"Get closer!" Cedar shouts.

Um, Carl is trying to step on my toes, Cedar. *You* get closer!

But I bite back my totally reasonable objections and step closer, waving my arms up over my head like I'm one of those inflatable men at car dealerships. And then Carl Freburg spins around, swinging his meaty pink elbow directly into my chin. There's just . . . impact.

One second I'm avoiding a butt and the next I'm sitting on mine, and my jaw hurts and those awful fluorescent lights seem even brighter and I taste *blood*.

I know that taste because I bit my tongue once. I was never the same again. It was like I grew up too fast that day. You can just . . . *bite yourself*!?

Cedar comes charging past me in a blur. Then there is shouting and cursing and I look over to see Cedar and Carl Freburg rolling around in a tangle of arms and legs. Coach tries to separate them. Mo grabs Carl's left sneaker and pulls it off for some reason. I want to help, but in fairness, I've just suffered head trauma.

Coach finally tears my brother free and pushes him back.

"Enough!" Coach shouts.

Everyone freezes. Mo is still holding Carl's shoe.

"Apologize!" Coach bellows, gesturing wildly at everyone.

"Sorry," I murmur.

Coach rolls his eyes. "Not you, Green. Carl . . . apologize to Green."

"Cedar just attacked me, Coach!" Carl protests.

"Now!"

Carl Freburg gives me a new look. It cannot be confused with cheese in the teeth. It's a look of pure hatred. I take a step back . . . I am really not enjoying basketball tryouts so far.

"Sorry, Green," Carl says, but it's more of a hiss than anything.

Cedar is eyeing him, hands clenching and unclenching at his sides. He looks like he wants to tackle Carl again, and Coach steps between them, eyeing my brother disapprovingly.

"Cedar, why don't you take Green home for the day?" Coach says. "Let everyone cool off."

"Fine," Cedar snaps, still glaring at Carl. "C'mon, Green."

Carl looks around. "Really? No apology for me? He kneed me in the balls, Coach—"

I don't hear the rest. I follow Cedar to the locker room and it's completely silent as we switch to our outdoor clothes. The Croc-socks feel amazing. It's like wearing rubber clouds.

I glance at my brother, who's trembling so much he's struggling with his laces.

"You just saved Carl Freburg's life," I say. "I was about to force-choke him."

Cedar stares at me for a moment. Then he bursts out laughing and slings his arm around my shoulder, pulling me in for a noogie. It's my least favorite brother activity, but I let it slide today.

"Let's go home, little bro," Cedar says, scooping up his backpack.

"Cedar?"

"Yeah?"

"Do you think I could get a mouth guard before next try-out?" I pause, thinking about Carl Freburg and that ill-placed knee. "And maybe a cup?"

Cedar laughs again. "We'll talk to Dad."

CHaPteR 4

CEDAR

"I told you this was a bad idea," Mom says between bites, glaring across the table at me.

My mom has the world's foremost death stare. That thing can stop traffic. She's a vet and is super good with animals. People . . . not so much. The ironic thing is that we don't even have any pets, since Dad is allergic to pet hair.

I'm super jealous of Mo: He has *two* cats. I love cats. I've probably watched every cat video on the Internet, which is saying something. If the NBA doesn't work out, I'm going to be a vet too. Well, if I can get my math grades up. Honestly, pro basketball might be more likely.

I try that smile with the extra cheeks again . . . but she just death-stares it into oblivion.

"It was Carl Freburg's fault," I say reflexively.

Coach called home to tell my parents about the fight. It's kind of lame, but he was also checking in on Green's jaw, so I'll cut him some slack for that.

Green is sitting to my left, finishing his cheese and mayo sandwich. He's lucky. We're having fish sticks today and I would totally go for a sandwich instead, but Mom says I have to eat "whatever the rest of the family is having." Double standards much?

"So you took your first-ever punch, huh, Green?" Dad says. "How'd it feel?"

Green moves his jaw around. "I didn't love it."

"It's good for you," Dad says, miming some boxing moves. As usual, he is wearing a Spandex shirt that looks like it's one solid pec flex away from exploding. I take after him more than Mom in the looks department (other than the muscles, unfortunately): white skin, brown hair, brown eyes, and big, protruding ears like twin satellite dishes. "Now you're a real heavyweight. The lean, green fighting machine."

"Nice," I say, and Dad and I exchange props.

"Well, one tryout was enough," Mom says curtly. "Experiment over."

I frown, my fork pausing in midair. "He's going to make the cut, Mom."

"It doesn't matter!" she snaps. "He got *punched*, Cedar!"

"It was technically an elbow—" Green starts, but he too is silenced by the death stare.

Mom shakes her head. "It's too dangerous."

"They're not base-jumping, dear," Dad says. "It's just basketball."

"This Carl Freburg boy has always caused problems for Green," she replies, her cheeks flushing. I got Dad's looks, but Mom's temper. "He knows that Green has a neurological disorder—"

"Here we go," I mutter.

"It's called Asperger's syndrome," Mom says loudly. "And social activities are—"

I throw my hands up in exasperation. "You're right! Let's just lock Green in his room and throw away the key. That way he'll never have to interact with human beings ever again."

"Would I have the PlayStation—" Green says, but this time I give him the look.

Mom points her index finger at me. "Cedar, your brother—"

"Is perfectly normal!" I shout back. "His only problem is that *you* baby him."

Okay, now I've done it. The death stare is gone. There is just . . . silence.

Mom and I have had the argument about how much she babies Green a few times—okay, a hundred times—and it never ends well.

Dad is looking between us like he's weighing if he'll try to save me or just settle into a quieter life with one child.

"I'm okay, Mom," Green says. He hates disagreeing with Mom—I do it enough for both of us—so I'm surprised he's chiming in. "I want to go to the next tryout . . . if I make it."

Mom looks just as surprised. She keeps glancing at me like I'm feeding Green lines on a cue card or something. Then she just scowls and goes back to her fish sticks.

"Fine," she snaps. "But if something happens to Green . . . it's on you, Cedar."

Green frowns. "How dangerous is this sport?"

"You'll be fine," I manage, trying not to sound too relieved that I haven't been grounded for the next three hundred years. "Green had a great tryout. Sort of."

I hear my cell phone pinging from the living room—Mom banned it from the kitchen table a few months ago because apparently I was forgetting to eat and talk to them and stuff. I glance longingly toward it, then at my awful charred fish sticks, then at the living room again.

Mom sighs. "Go."

I load my plate into the dishwasher and run for my phone, finding some messages from Mo about the fight and Meghan Hayes saying:

OMG I HEARD

I check my newest TikTok video again and feel my whole body deflate. Ninety likes. A total flop. I collapse onto the couch and start messaging Mo back. I also "like" Keesha's newest video and add a handclap/fire/heart emoji comment.

The heart might have been a bit much, but I totally love her. We haven't spoken yet or anything, but I can just tell.

I watch Keesha's video again, thinking. It's one of those viral dances. Maybe Mo was right. Maybe we do need a dance. But how to stand out? What if I dance and then shoot a three and then, you know, dance again or something? Or . . . what if I make a *basketball dance*.

Whoa.

I quickly shoot Mo a message:

Cedar: We have homework.

Mo: Yeah I know did Green help you with yours yet? What did he get for question 8?

39

Cedar: No we're making a basketball dance. Think of some ideas. I'll FaceTime you in an hour.

Mo: SICK

Mo: But seriously what did he get?

I sigh. Mo won't talk to Green directly, but he's not above using Green's powers for evil.

"Green!"

"Fro-Mo, I'm telling you . . . it should be shimmy, shimmy, *then* shake as the ball rolls down the shoulders."

Mo picks at his front teeth thoughtfully. It looks like they had broccoli for dinner tonight.

We're FaceTiming and he's safely locked away in his bedroom . . . his parents are even less supportive of his social media career than mine. His dad told him he was going to throw his phone in the lake if he gets another *Satisfactory* on his report card.

"I prefer shimmy, step, arm flair, shake," Mo says, demonstrating as he talks.

He caps it off by releasing the basketball from his outstretched right hand. It's supposed to roll behind his craned neck and into his waiting left palm . . . but the ball hits him in the ear and bounces away instead.

We are having serious choreography issues.

"Let's try it my way first," I say. "And dude: *Lean your head forward.*"

Mo rubs the back of his neck, grimacing. "I'm sore, bro. It's been, like, two hours."

"We're almost there. Now on three. One, two . . . "

"Can we do one arm flair?" Mo asks.

"What is you with you and arm flairs!"

There is a soft knock at my bedroom door. Only one person knocks like that.

"Call you back," I say, ending the call.

I pull my door open and find Green standing in the hallway. His cheeks are rosy and his knobby shoulders are hunched forward. I instinctively check his left hand.

Yep. Bouncy ball.

"You good?" I ask, concerned.

"Can I come in?"

I gesture to the bed. "Take a seat."

Green shuffles over and plops onto the mattress, staring down at his navy blue socks. I despise those socks . . . they make his scarlet Crocs look even more ridiculous. If that's possible.

"Did you lose at Minecraft again?" I ask suspiciously.

"No." Green pauses. "Well, yes. But I was distracted. Listen . . . I think maybe I shouldn't go back, Cedar. Even if I make it. Which I definitely won't because I'm awful. But either way."

I sit down beside him on the bed, leaning forward to try to make eye contact. "Why?"

"Nobody wants me there."

"Carl Freburg is a meat stick—" I start.

"Mo doesn't either. And, well, everyone. Coach only invited me because of you."

"No, he invited you because you have potential."

Green rolls the ball around in his palm, still not looking at me. "Potential for what?"

"To be a great player! And, you know, to make some friends."

"I don't need friends," Green says sullenly.

"Everyone needs friends. I mean, you've got me, but one or two others couldn't hurt."

Green points at his jaw. "It can definitely hurt!"

"Not Carl. He's a dink."

I pat his left knee, which is doing that thing where it bounces a mile a minute. I'm not sure if it's nervousness or just force of habit, but when he does it at the dinner table it's like a minor earthquake. Plates legit start to rattle.

He's already wearing his flannel Star Wars pajamas, of course. He's worn them every night since he was six, and his skinny ankles and wrists are growing more exposed by the day.

"This is going to be awesome, Green," I continue, leaning even farther to try to make eye contact. I'm going to faceplant off the bed pretty soon. "Trust me. Don't listen to Mom. She just babies you because you're the youngest."

"She doesn't baby me," he mutters.

"Dude, she calls you her Little Greenie sometimes."

"That's . . ." Green sighs. "Yeah."

"Let's just check the list at lunch tomorrow and go from there. Cool?"

Green hesitates. "Cool." He starts for the door, then looks back. "Why are you so sweaty?"

"We're attempting a basketball dance. I'm tentatively calling it the Hoop Scoot Boogie."

Green shakes his head. "Good night, Cedar."

"Night, little bro."

I listen to him shuffle down the hallway and then call Mo back. He answers right away, but he's sitting in front of his massive bedroom TV holding an Xbox controller. With both cats in his lap. Ugh. He's so lucky.

"Dude . . . is that Fortnite?" I ask incredulously. "I was gone for two minutes."

"I didn't know how long you would be!"

"Stay focused! And hi, Fluffy and Boots!" I say, my voice instantly going weird like it always does when I talk to his cats. "Give them a head-scratch for me, will you? Oh, and by the way . . . why did you take Carl's shoe during our fight? Green told me you yanked it off his foot."

"I was neutralizing his wrestling stance, bro! You get no traction in socks."

"That . . . makes sense actually." I prop my phone against the base of the wall and get back into position. Then another thought strikes me. "Listen, I need you to stand up for Green too. If I'm busy, I'm relying on you to watch out for him."

"He's not my brother—"

"Promise me, Fro-Mo."

"I promise," he mutters, but he sounds so reluctant that I feel a flush of annoyance.

"What is your problem with Green?" I demand. "Seriously."

"Dude, I thought we were dancing."

"We can dance later! You told me you were going to be cool. What's the deal?"

Mo is pointedly facing away from the camera now. "I don't know."

"Mo . . ."

"He doesn't talk! And he's just, like . . . sitting alone all the time. I don't know what to say to him! I'm sure he's nice and I know he's your little brother, but c'mon, man, he's weird—"

"He's not weird!" I snap. "And lower your voice . . . you're upsetting the cats."

Mo scowls. "Whatever. You're the one who told me he has assburger—"

"It's a P sound," I snap.

I never should have said anything. Mo asked me one day why Green was so quiet, and I said he had, well, maybe *assburger syndrome* because I didn't know how to say it correctly at the time. And now it's like I gave Mo a scientific excuse to ignore Green.

"It would just be nice if my two bros could get along, you know?" I say. "And by that, I entirely mean you being nicer to Green."

"Why can't Green try to be more normal?" he demands.

"What does that even mean? He's just as normal as anyone else. Except way cooler."

We glare at each other for a moment, and then he sets the phone down on the mattress and starts playing Fortnite. I am now looking directly up his nose, which is a *massive* breach of FaceTime etiquette. He's not even pointing me at the TV. This is some next-level pettiness.

"So that's how you're going to be, huh?" I say.

"I don't want to dance anymore. My neck hurts."

"You just remember your promise. When Green is on the team—"

Mo snorts. "Your brother sucks, man. He's not going to be on the team."

"I think you need to cool off."

"You cool off!" he shouts.

I end the call and throw my phone on the bed. I can't wait until Green proves everyone wrong. My mom and Mo and stupid, smelly Carl Freburg. Two months on the team and Green will be Mr. Popularity.

He just has to make the first cut. I chew on my fingernail, thinking.

Maybe I need to talk to Coach again.

CHAPTER 5

GREEN

I lie in bed, rolling my trusty red bouncy ball around in my hand. I've already listened to Dad wake up and leave; the faint hiss of the shower, the ten-second tornado of the blender, the beep of his unlocking car doors and the baritone rumble as he drives away.

Mom is next to leave; her shower is done, the hissing kettle has clicked, and I heard her bedroom door close as she went to change out of her housecoat. Cedar is still asleep in the room next to me, mumbling about upsetting someone named . . . Fluffy? I have no idea what he is talking about.

I roll the ball up to my fingers and back down into my cupped palm. My body doesn't like being still. Sometimes my legs shake. Sometimes my toes scrunch up in my Crocs. Mom says she read that it's called *stimming*, and it's common in kids with autism spectrum disorders. She was worried about it, but I told her it actually makes me feel better. Sometimes it's nice to focus on something I can control.

I think *autism* is a neat word. It basically means *isolated self*. A Swiss guy named Eugen Blueler came up with the term and spared a whole lot of kids from being Bluelers.

I remember another parent once asked my mom, "Oh . . . is Green *autistic*?" It was like it was a bad word. Like I had a disease or something. But I've met other kids on the spectrum and I have to say . . . they all seem pretty happy. Including me.

Sure, I would like to be named Gale. Or Aragorn. Oh man. That would be so awesome. *Aragorn Bennett*. I could have a cool sword and nobody would even question it.

"Hey, Little Greenie," my mom says, poking her head through the doorway.

"Hey, Mom."

She sits down on my bed. Her hair is pulled back into a messy bun, her sky-blue scrubs peeking out beneath a thick wool sweater. She lays her hand over mine, gently squeezing my fingers to keep the ball from rolling around.

"You know what Dr. Lee says," she reminds me.

"That I should try relaxing without my coping mechanisms," I say.

Dr. Lee always has suggestions for me. But he's a family physician, not an Asperger's specialist, so Mom doesn't listen to all of them.

I think that's why she's so excited about seeing this Dr. Shondez. Mom says Dr. Shondez can tell us if I really do need extra help . . . and how much. That's what worries me. Never mind the pills and private schools. What if she says, "This butt sandwich needs a white padded room."

I squeeze my bouncy ball, feeling a wave of panic.

Mom must guess my train of thought, because she says, "The appointment will be fine, Green."

"I don't want to go," I say for the tenth time.

"We have to go," she replies. "Let's just hear what she has to say."

I look away, but she takes my chin and gently guides me back to her.

"How did you sleep?" she asks.

I can smell the peppermint toothpaste on her breath. I like the smell. If it wasn't for the sneezing, I'd switch to peppermint in an instant.

"I dreamed that a giant basketball ate me like Pac-Man," I murmur.

She smiles. "I'm proud of you."

"No, like, it actually ate me—"

"*For trying out.* I know I'm not being very supportive. I just worry about you, Greenie."

"I know," I say, watching the morning sunlight play across her face.

It's funny. Dr. Lee said I would always have a hard time connecting with people. But I connect with Cedar and Dad and Mom. I can almost sense what Mom's thinking just by looking at her eyes.

So . . . maybe I just focus on the people I love. And I'm fine with that.

"But you went," Mom says. "And even if you don't make the cut . . . your father and I are both very proud of you." She leans down and kisses my forehead. "See you tonight, Green."

I listen to her footsteps on the stairs. Her car thrumming to life. The slow tread of tires on the waking street. And I roll the ball around in my palm until Cedar's alarm goes off, and he groans, "There's no way," and slaps the snooze button.

I smile and go to wake him up.

"Whoa," I whisper, looking at Cedar in disbelief. "I made the cut."

"Yeah," he whispers. He grips my shoulders and gives me a shake. "Way to go, Green!"

I read my name again, as if to confirm that it really is up there. Below the list of fifteen names is the information for the next tryout: tomorrow at five p.m., which is kind of strange.

"Five o'clock on a Friday?" I say, frowning.

It's not like I had big plans for the weekend, though five to six *is* my daily hour of PlayStation. I know a one-hour limit might sound strict, but I once played for nine straight hours during summer break. Mom went to work and came home and I literally hadn't moved. Not even to *pee.* It was an awesome day, but I can see how it might have been unhealthy.

Cedar shrugs. "Coach said the senior girls team grabbed the afterschool spot first. No big deal. We can go home, get a little extra practice in, then come back."

"I just hope Mom adjusts my PlayStation hour," I murmur.

Around us, the whole range of human emotions is on display. Jerome is doing a celebratory Fortnite dance. Brooks looks almost as surprised to be on there as I am and keeps reading the names again. "I . . . made the cut?" he keeps whispering.

And Carl Freburg?

"Is this a joke?" Carl hisses, pushing his way through the group to glare at the list.

Carl was a starter on the team last year. Cedar says he fouled out of, like, half the games, but was still the third leading scorer.

I frown and read the list again. Carl Freburg isn't on there.

Uh-oh.

Carl stares at the list for a while. Then he slowly turns to face me, his right eye twitching. I wonder if it's a neurological issue, but he also might just be very angry.

Cedar steps forward even as the rest of the boys step back . . . except Mo, who sighs.

"Stupid promises," Mo mutters.

I have no idea what he is talking about.

Focus, Green. There is a potential assailant ready to . . . assail you. I wish I was actually a ninja. I doubt Mom would let me have ninja stars because, you know, all the stabby metal parts, but maybe I can talk her into nunchuks?

But Carl Freburg doesn't attack.

"Coach is such a tool," he mutters, then storms down the hallway, huffing like a steam engine.

Cedar lets out a sigh of relief. "Okay, bro, so we're going to shoot around tonight—"

"Green," an unnecessarily loud voice cuts in.

I whirl around and see Coach poking his head out of his classroom. He also teaches seventh-grade geography.

"Can I speak with you for a second?" Coach says.

I look at Cedar in alarm. Did he change his mind already? I didn't even get to stress out yet.

But he's still just waiting there expectantly, so I follow him into the classroom while Cedar plays sentry at the door.

It's recess, so the classroom is empty. Coach flips one of the students' chairs around to face his desk, and I awkwardly take a seat, staring at the floor.

"Surprised?" Coach asks, settling in behind his desk.

I look up, but not all the way to his eyes, settling instead on the diamond ring dangling from a chain around his neck. He always reminds me of Frodo in *The Lord of the Rings* except Frodo was fairly quiet and, oops, Coach is still staring at me.

"Yes," I say.

"Well, let's be honest with each other. It wasn't a great tryout. Even before the incident."

I nod. No point arguing that one.

"But Cedar is a great player, and technically you have the same DNA."

"With some exceptions," I murmur.

Coach lowers his head, even tilting it sideways a little, obviously trying to catch my eye. "You have potential, Green. But I can't put you on the team unless you show some significant improvement tomorrow. Cedar says you two are going to practice. Just show me that you're trying and I'll find a spot for you. Deal?"

I nod again even though I have no idea how to prove that I've "been trying." Photos? Should I give him a sweaty sock? Am

I actually supposed to get better in twenty-four hours?

Coach dips his head even lower, forcing his stubbled chin into my view, so my eyes go from him to the framed picture on his desk. It's Coach, I'm guessing his wife, and a girl about Cedar's age with a big, toothy grin and short auburn hair. Coach seems to follows my gaze.

"My little one," he says fondly, scooping up the photo. "Well . . . not so little anymore. Abby. She's in tenth grade already, if you can believe it."

I'm not sure why I wouldn't believe it—does he have a reason to lie?—so I just nod.

Coach sighs and leans back in his chair, taking the picture with him. He holds it in front of him with one hand while the other plays with the ring. I want to leave, but he looks like one of those pesky sad faces I always struggled to pick out. Possibly also constipated.

Mom would say something supportive, but nothing comes to mind, so I just support by sitting.

"Funny how time works, huh?" Coach says. "How some things can feel like they happened yesterday and a hundred years ago at the same time. I feel like we were just taking our baby girl to the zoo, and now Abby is staying out past curfew and dating idiots. One of them ate two bags of chips yesterday while I was at the gym. Abby says she ate them, but it was *two bags*. I know there was a boy over." He shakes his head. "Abby and I just can't seem to get along lately. She's always in a bad mood when she's home. Renee would have known what to do."

I have absolutely no idea what he's talking about, but I just nod again because that seems to be working.

"I keep Renee close, of course," Coach continues, patting the wedding ring. "That's all you can do." Then he clears his throat and puts the picture back. "Anyway, put some work in, son. I'm pulling for you. You know what . . . you're a good guy to talk to. Very attentive listener."

Well, that's true. I just nod again and retreat back to the hallway. As I leave, I glance back and see Coach pick up the photo again. He looks . . . sad. He must really miss his wife.

I guess I know what it's like to miss someone. I miss Oma every day.

"Well?" Cedar demands from his post beside the door, looking up from his phone.

"I'm still on the team," I confirm. "He just wants me to practice before Friday."

Cedar shoots me a lopsided grin. "Oh, we are going to practice all right. I already have a plan. Five hundred layups made. One hundred free throws. Fifty threes . . . that one might take a while. We'll also do some serious dribbling work when we get home—"

He keeps talking as we head outside for recess, but I start to space out. I can't believe I actually made the first cut. It cost me a sore jaw and provided new motivation for my apparent archnemesis, Carl Freburg, but I'm basically a professional athlete now. Maybe I'll get a leather jacket, too.

Actually, no . . . leather somehow gets too cold *and* too hot, so it's really only ideal for fall and spring. I wear one hundred percent polyester for my outerwear. It's the all-season fabric.

"And then we'll do some push-ups before bed and—" Cedar is saying.

I look at him, frowning. I'm not sure I like where this is going.

CHAPTER 6

CEDAR

Green hits a three-pointer. I repeat: Green hits a *three-pointer*. It's just the warm-up around the pylons and no one is guarding him or anything, but it still feels like the unlikeliest bucket in the entire history of basketball. We practiced for a long time yesterday, and it's already paying off.

I stop halfway through the pylons, shouting, "Make it rain, Green!"

Green flashes a shy grin and goes after the ball.

I turn to Mo, who was forced to an abrupt stop behind me. We're probably causing some serious traffic issues, but Coach is busy yelling at Andrew Staff and hasn't noticed yet.

"Well?" I say, smirking.

"Dude, my ayeeyo can hit a three with enough tries," Mo says, rolling his eyes.

"Your ayeeyo is a beast. She did thirty push-ups at your birthday party, remember?"

He pauses. "She is a bit of a show-off, isn't she? Still. It was one shot."

But I am already off again, dribbling through the zigzagging pylons as I cross up imaginary defenders.

I started playing ball when I was five, after Dad bought me a hoop for Christmas. It's still sitting at the top of my driveway, but with a mud-stained, slightly cracked Plexiglas backboard and a fraying orange-and-blue net that I use to hang off to try to dunk.

I tried out for the Palmerston Panthers junior team in sixth grade, just like Green, and I made it easily. I was already tall and I'd been shooting around in the driveway for years, so I was the best player on the team from day one. And, well, my whole life changed.

I know that sounds melodramatic, but I was pretty shy. . . . I really only spoke to Mo before that. Before I knew it, I was friends with the whole team, and I was going to everyone's birthday parties, and I could even talk to girls without breaking into hives, which was a nice development.

For me, basketball led straight to popularity. And now it's Green's turn to follow suit.

I pull up at the free-throw line and take a jump shot just as Coach blows his whistle.

Swish.

"Scrimmage time!" Coach bellows.

He starts divvying us up, running around and pointing wildly in one direction or the other—it really is a good thing he takes that chain off. The guy is a total hazard.

"Brooks you're on B, Corrado . . . A, Cedar . . . A, Green . . . B. Where is Mo!?"

"Right behind you, Coach," Mo says, flinching and raising a hand.

"You're on A!"

Mo sighs and wipes some Coach spit off his cheek. Oh, Coach spits when he yells.

I look around, concerned. All of the best players are on Team A. I suspect they're the ones who are already on the team: Me, Mo, Andrew, and Corrado were all starters last year, and a few of the other mainstays are there as well.

That means Green is definitely on the chopping block.

Green is sipping his water bottle by the bench, staring at the student-drawn pictures scattered around the gym like he's a collector of fine crayon artwork or something. I look him over, sighing.

He's way too skinny. I'm skinny too, but Green is one moderate breeze away from taking flight. His knees look like globs of partially chewed gum holding two uncooked breadsticks together.

Maybe I can convince him to double up on his cheese slices or use extra-starchy bread. I wonder if they make protein powder mayo. . . . I'll have to ask Dad.

Green managed two push-ups this morning. *Two*.

"You ready, bro?" I say, sticking my fist out to him for props.

Green lightly taps my knuckles. He consider props a "unnecessary risk of bone bruises."

"I guess so," he says, shrugging.

"Love the confidence. Try not to get Muay Thai'd today."

Green sighs. "Dad forgot to pick me up a mouth g Then he offered me *his* cup. Ew."

"You'll be fine," I assure him.

"Cedar, I have adult teeth now. If I lose those, they are *not* coming back."

I give him an extra-wide smile and point at my mouth. "Still got mine."

"For now," he grumbles.

Coach's whistle blasts through the air, and the pivotal second scrimmage begins.

Green and I are technically both centers, but I play a lot of small forward and even shooting guard so that I can control the ball more. As a result, I am matched up against Brooks, while Green is on Corrado, who is really good but thankfully less violent than Carl Freburg.

I'm kind of playing two games since I'm both trying to score coach/monitor Green, and my game is suffering as a result. get blocked by Brooks at one point, which is humiliating, e's, like, four-foot-seven with his shoes on. Mo almost he's laughing so hard.

t him as I inbound the ball. We are already on the s don't laugh at bros. But Mo doesn't even have the k embarrassed. He just glares right back at me. sn't even pass me the ball on the next possession. etting real.

is that Green is doing pretty well. He's get- and he even scores a few layups on the n safely go back to balling, and I make a oks for an easy layup of my own.

r, I notice that Green is *way* out of

"Green . . . get your head in the game!" Coach snaps.

Green flinches and runs up the court on offense . . . and then forgets to set a screen. Or put his hand up for the ball. Or try to rebound the missed jump shot.

Uh-oh. I know that glazed look. Green is spacing out. Hard. I can never quite figure out what triggers it, but Green just floats off sometimes. It can be mid-conversation. Over dinner. It could be on a *roller coaster*. I've seen it.

"What happened to pick-and-rolls!" Coach shouts. "Green . . . *do something*!"

Coach is pulling his hair. That's a bad sign. He's already lost most of it.

But Green is definitely still spacing.

Sure enough, Green forgets to run back on the next defensive possession. Corrado is left wide open on the block, and Mo passes him the ball for the world's easiest bucket. Green's teammates groan.

I'm about to say something encouraging . . . but Coach reacts first.

"What was that?" Coach screams, storming onto the court. His face is so red I think he might blow a gasket. "We play defense on this team, Green! I told you to show me something."

Coach stops right in front of Green's face, poking a finger at his chest.

"What are you doing out there?" he demands. "Are you daydreaming?"

"Yes," Green murmurs.

Of course he does. Even in the face of imminent danger, he's still Green.

"Can you look at me when I'm talking to you?" Coach says.

I see Green's left hand fumbling for his shorts, but these ones have no pockets, so no bouncy ball. I move to intervene . . . but not before my endlessly honest brother replies once again.

"No," Green says.

"Then you can get out of here!" Coach bellows, spit flying everywhere.

Green's pale eyes go wide, his left hand freezing at his side with nothing to hold on to.

"Coach!" I shout, stepping between them and shielding my little brother.

But I'm too late. Green sniffs and runs for the locker room. I can hear some of the guys laughing as he disappears through the double doors.

I turn back to Coach, trembling with anger. *"Not cool, Coach."*

He waves a hand in dismissal. "I'm just trying to whip him into shape—"

"You need to chill out," I snap, and a part of me is like, *Dude, you're talking to a teacher.* But the big brother part of me is in charge now . . . and that Cedar would fight a bear for Green.

Coach stares at me, his eyes twitching. Am I going to have to fight *Coach*?

"Go talk to your brother," Coach finally snaps. "And take the rest of the tryout off."

"I will," I say. "I might take a while off, actually. Like the whole season."

And with that last, dramatic threat, I storm toward the gym doors.

Mo looks like he's about to faint. He's mouthing, "Season?"

It was a bit much. I definitely don't want to sit out the entire season, but I really am mad at Coach. He knows Green is shy. And he still screamed in his face in front of the whole team.

It's going to take a long time to get Green's confidence up again, and I've been working on his self-esteem for *years*. Checking the locker room, I see that Green's backpack is already gone.

I quickly change my shoes and hurry after him.

CHapTER 7

GREEN

I like September. It's cool but not cold, and there's no confusing Daylight Savings Time yet when it gets dark at five and I want to fall asleep during dinner. That's especially nice because it's already almost six o'clock. . . . I don't think I've ever walked home from school this late.

I also love the fall leaves. I think it's interesting that they get *more* beautiful when they get old. That is definitely not how humans work. I've seen pictures of my Opa when he was younger, and he was a handsome guy. He looks like a potato now.

But I can't enjoy the leaves today. First of all, it must have rained during tryouts because everything is soaked, and I stepped in mud when I was leaving the school. When you're wearing Croc-socks, mud is a big deal.

And more importantly, Coach just yelled at me. Like a true dressing-down. I've been yelled at before, but never publicly, and never with so much spittle. It was like standing in a disappointed monsoon. To be honest, it made me angry. Did I really deserve to get *screamed at?*

And I could see the other players laughing and making jokes. I think they were all just waiting for me to mess up. They were thrilled that Coach was finally getting rid of the weird kid.

The worst part is I thought I was doing pretty good. I got three scores! I mean, who cares how many the other team gets? When Cedar and I play we cheer when the other person scores. It just seems like a friendlier system.

We also talk about video games and stuff and sometimes I explain the plot of a movie we watched the night before because he was on his phone the whole time. And, well, I guess I thought there was more of that.

"Green."

Cedar runs up and carefully checks me over like maybe I was crying. I'm not. I actually don't cry very much, which sounds super tough, but Dr. Lee said it's because kids with Asperger's can be "emotionally detached." Honestly, I can't do anything right for these doctors.

"Hey."

"You okay?" he asks as we turn onto the shortcut through Palmerston Park.

There's a winding concrete footpath that leads through the park to our street . . . it's only about a twenty-minute walk to school. That's pretty short except for in January and February when it feels like twenty hours. Once I got so cold my fingers started *burning*. It was very confusing.

I keep my eyes on my feet. I've got my navy blue socks on again, partially visible through the holes in my bright red Crocs. Cedar says the color combination makes his eyes hurt.

"Fine," I murmur, because I think he's still waiting for an answer.

"I told Coach he needs to chill out. It was both liberating and terrifying."

I try to smile, but I can't manage it. I guess I'm more upset than I realized. I'm officially cut. I let Cedar down, and we won't get to hang out after school anymore. The team practices or plays four days a week. That means I'm going to have to walk home alone every day but Tuesday and bounce the rubber ball by myself.

Cedar pulls me to a stop. "Green, talk to me."

"What?" I manage.

"That wasn't okay. Coach is going to apologize."

"No—"

"Yes, he will . . . or I will sit out the entire season in semi-peaceful protest. Semi-peaceful because I kind of want to egg his car, and I need to keep my options open."

I frown. "While I agree that throwing eggs is far better than eating them, you need to play, Cedar. Give it up. I have clearly been cut."

"Not necessarily—"

"Cedar. I'm cut."

He looks at me for a moment. "It's all going to work out, little bro. I promise."

"What's going to work out?"

"Everything!" he says, throwing his hands up. "Ball and school and friends—"

I shake my head and start walking again. "I don't need any friends, Cedar."

"That's what everyone says until they have them! Friends are great. You'll love them."

He doesn't get it. I know he means well, but I really don't care if Mo or Corrado or Brooks likes me.

"Green," Cedar says.

"What?"

"Incoming!"

I whirl around just as a bouncy ball comes hurtling through the air toward me, rocketing off the bike path and heading for the rain-cloud sky. Cedar must have had one on him today too.

I know I'm supposed to be wallowing, but it's a *bouncy ball*. I try to grab it, miss, and then burst out laughing as it flies past me, careening down the path.

When I finally retrieve it, Cedar is still, like, a hundred feet away, waving for me to throw it back. I chuck the bouncy ball toward him, and even though it's wet outside, we play the greatest game on earth until our arms are sore. Then we start home together, and I forget all about the stupid basketball tryout.

That is, until we get home and find Coach standing on our front porch.

Coach whirls toward me, his face purple with rage. *"Where is it?"*

CHAPTER 8

CEDAR

I look back and forth from Coach to Green, confused. Green fumbles for his bouncy ball.

"What are you talking about, Coach—" I start.

"My ring!" Coach cuts in, spit flying again. "It's gone. Stolen right off my desk!"

Our front door is wide open, and I can see Mom hurrying back from the kitchen with her phone pressed against her ear. She was probably about to call my cell, because when she sees us she puts the phone away and comes out onto the porch. Green is still rigid, eyes down, and I know that's just Green . . . but he *looks* guilty.

"No one would steal your ring, Coach," I say uncertainly. "That's ridiculous."

"Green stole it!" Coach snaps, leveling an accusing finger at him. "And I want it back."

My mom steps closer to Coach, one eyebrow dangerously raised. "Easy, Coach."

Coach looks at Mom and takes a step back, some of the color draining from his cheeks.

"Green was the only one there," Coach sputters.

"Where?" I ask.

"The gym office," Coach says. "When I told him to leave . . ." He shoots another nervous look at my mom. "Well, I mean, when he left the tryout, the rest of the school was completely empty. It was almost six o'clock on a Friday . . . even the teachers were gone. The only other person left in the entire school was Maggie."

Maggie is our school janitor, and she is infamously mean. I heard Andrew Staff once got caught spraying a juice box at someone and she mopped him. Like . . . she used a *mop* on his *head*. I think that's assault, but she didn't get fired.

I assume Principal Nickel was too afraid of her to try.

"Wasn't the office door locked?" Mom says.

Coach scowls. "I never lock any doors in that school. I don't even bring my keys most days. I'm never the first one there in the morning and Maggie always locks up after basketball. And I never thought anyone would sneak into the gym office!"

He tries to compose himself, taking a deep, shaky breath.

"Listen, I acted inappropriately when I yelled at Green, and I apologize. But everyone knows what that ring means to me. I just want it back." His voice wavers at the end, and despite the fact that he's accusing my little brother of theft, I still feel bad. It sounds like he's close to tears. *"Please."*

My mom and I both turn to Green. He has his hands clasped at his stomach, the left one holding the bouncy ball, the right one wringing and fidgeting and trying hard to keep them both together.

He really does look guilty. *Is* he guilty?

Green would have walked right by Coach's office on the way out of the gym. If the wedding ring was sitting there, and he was mad enough, well . . . it was possible.

Green used to have a pretty serious temper himself. He's been a lot calmer the last year or two, but I've seen him fired up. He'd slam doors. Scream. Cry. He even tried to run away from home a couple of times growing up because Dad asked him to eat a celery stick or Mom told him to turn his video games off.

"I don't have it," he mumbles.

"Don't have it!?" Coach erupts. "Let me see that backpack—"

"Don't . . . touch . . . his . . . bag," Mom warns, her voice very low. "He just told you he didn't steal it." She takes Green's shoulder and ushers him inside, death-staring Coach on the way. "I'm sure the ring was just misplaced. Maybe Maggie accidentally vacuumed it up—"

"Maggie didn't even do the gym office yet," Coach protests. "Or my classroom. And I checked them both . . . trust me. I even called Layne to give me a hand. Mrs. Bennett, Green was the only one left in the school who could have taken it. The rest of the boys were with me. Well, I suppose Cedar left early, but obviously *he* didn't take it."

"Why not?" Mom says quietly.

I know that voice. She uses it when I do something *bad*. Coach is in dangerous waters.

He scratches the back of his neck, looking nervous. "Well . . . uh . . . he's been on the team for years."

"And because he doesn't have *Asperger's syndrome*," Mom snaps. "Is that it?"

Coach looks like he is about to be death-stared into oblivion, so I intervene.

"I didn't take your ring, Coach," I say. "And neither did Green. It will turn up."

I try to keep any uncertainty out of my voice.

"If I could just check Green's backpack—" Coach starts again.

Mom cuts him off. "It's time to go, Coach. *I* will speak to Green. But I also trust him."

Coach just stands there for a moment. I remember last year when he lost the ring during our game at Pringle Creek . . . he went completely ballistic. He turned the whole school upside down, and it wasn't even our school. He found the ring under the bleachers eventually, but he was legit in tears by then.

I know what that ring means to him.

"Just have Green return it to me," Coach finally manages, shuffling to his car. "Please."

He drives off, and I turn to Green, who is digging his toe into the hardwood.

I know he said he didn't take it. And it doesn't really sound like something Green would do. But Coach did scream in his face. And Green did have a few minutes alone before I caught up to him outside.

If Coach is right and there was no one else was in the entire school but Maggie, then . . . well, it looks bad. I feel like I have to ask.

"Green, did you take Coach's ring?" I ask quietly. "It's okay. We can just give it back."

Green's pale blue eyes go glassy. Then he storms upstairs.

• • •

I poke my head into Green's bedroom. It's pretty bare compared to mine. He has two framed pictures on the wall: a gray wolf and a bald eagle. Both were picked out by my mom. The walls are yellow with a cartoony spaceship trim along the top, which is super ugly, but Green seems to like it. It's been the exact same since he was born, I think.

There are a bunch of books on the shelf and even more piled into the little fort he made beneath his captain's bed, which has an open space behind the drawers. He used to go in there during thunderstorms or when Mom and Dad tried to get him to eat spaghetti. I think he's still got a spare pillow and blanket down there for emergencies. To this day, I have no idea what kind of emergency would be solved by sleeping under the bed.

He also keeps a spare jar of bouncy balls down there, just in case none of them survive the apocalypse.

Green is lying on his bed, reading another one of my mom's enormous detective novels. He already read all the kids' books he has so my Mom just gave up and let him have hers, even though there is some "questionable content that you should ignore, Green." I'm surprised he can hold that thing up in the air. He's also pointedly ignoring me.

I sigh and go sit next to him on the mattress. "What're you reading?"

"Go away."

Ignoring him, I slide backward to lean against the wall. "I was just checking, you know."

"Checking that I was both a thief *and* a liar? Thanks."

Hesitating, I glance at him. If he did take it, he might be embarrassed. Even afraid. I try to be as delicate as possible. "Well, I mean, Coach did yell at you. He kind of deserved it—"

Green lowers the book, glaring at me so hard he creates a sandy-blond unibrow.

"I didn't take it," he says.

I look at him for a moment, then feel a flash of guilt. This is my little brother—the most honest kid on earth. And here I am accusing him because he had a lot of meltdowns growing up? I'm as bad as Coach. "I believe you. I know that your nose grows if you lie."

"I *can* lie," Green says. "I just don't see the point. Now can you leave?"

He rolls over, tucking his knees in and expertly hiding his face behind the book.

"I'm sorry, okay?" I say. "It just sounded bad with the timing and everything."

Green is silent for a moment. "Everyone at school is going to think I took the ring."

"No, they're not. I'll tell them the truth."

"They'll think it anyway," Green whispers, his face still hidden. "Because it's me."

I reach over and pluck the book away. "What's that supposed to mean?"

"They already think I'm a weirdo, Cedar. Why do you think Coach assumed it was me right away? It could have just as easily been you . . . but he didn't even think about that, did he?"

I pause. "Well, that's because—"

"I have a mental disorder and you don't."

"You've been listening to Mom too much. You're perfectly normal."

"That's not what Dr. Lee says," he mutters. "He says I might need treatment. And this Dr. Shondez is probably going to tell me the same thing."

I catch a weird change in his voice. It's the same tone everyone in my house gets when they talk about Green's upcoming appointment. I have a distinct feeling they aren't telling me something important, but Green just changes the subject whenever I bring it up.

"Well, Dr. Lee is wrong," I reply simply. "Besides, who knows what normal is anyway? Mo dips his fries in ice cream."

"Ew."

"Exactly," I say. "And I do lots of weird stuff too. Like last night I had to cough, but it was such a big cough that I farted at the same time. That's never happened to me before, bro."

"How is that relevant?" Green says incredulously.

"I don't know. But it felt mad weird. It was like my whole body vibrated." I glance at him, smiling. "Listen, Coach is going to find the ring tomorrow. It probably just fell under his desk or something. And even if takes a day or two, nobody is going to blame you. Trust me."

Green still looks a bit skeptical, but he nods.

"Are we good?" I ask. "I can't have any fractures in our coniferous superteam."

"We're good," Green says, biting back a smile. "Now give me my book."

"Fine."

I hand him the book—that thing easily weighs five pounds—and head for the door.

"You really think people will believe me?" Green asks quietly.

"Absolutely," I assure him. "In fact, I bet you nobody else will even know the ring is missing."

I leave him to his reading and flop onto my own bed next door, pulling out my phone. All right—Instagram first for a few well-placed likes and maybe I'll post a story today. I stiffen.

There are six new DMs.

I open them up one by one, feeling my heart sinking.

Mo: yo just so you know I didn't spread the rumor Coach was yelling in the parking lot

Corrado: is it true?????????

Cherene: ummm this is kind of messed up

Brooks: not cool Tree.

Sylvia: REALLY CEDAR

Mo: Honestly though Tree . . . tell Green to give it back.

CHAPTER 9

GREEN

When I walk back into class after first break on Monday, everyone is staring at me. That happens sometimes, but not this bad. Even Mrs. Strachan is giving me a look like, Umm special shy boy, how come no one told me you were also a thief?!

It was fine first thing in the morning. But clearly the story spread around during break because when we got back inside after the bell it was officially stare-disapprovingly-at-Green time.

I *really* don't like being stared at, so I just bury my head in my hands, listening to Mrs. Strachan talk about Canadian geography. It sounds really big and empty and I wish I was there right now.

I had a good thing going. I was Green the Butt Sandwich and everyone ignored me. But no . . . I just *had* to try to be a normal kid. Now look at me. I'm a wanted felon.

I can just imagine the poster:

Green Bennett (yes, his name is actually Green). Stole Coach's dead wife's wedding ring because he got yelled at. Last seen sitting in his sixth-grade classroom. Wanted dead or alive. Preferably dead.

It doesn't make sense. Why would I take Coach's ring? I've never even stolen a pencil from school. Okay . . . once I accidentally packed a school eraser in my bag after art class, but I returned it first thing the next morning. Unless someone saw me take the eraser. . . . Oh no.

Do I have a criminal record!?

"Green . . . are you napping?" a familiar voice asks. Except also not familiar because it's a little . . . sharp. I look up. Mrs. Strachan is standing in front of me. She can be surprisingly sneaky.

"No."

She bends down, lowering her voice. "Anything you want to tell me?"

Not this again. Why can't people just be clear? I ponder the question. *Oh.* The ring.

"No."

She gives me a serious look of disapproval and chews on her bottom lip. She must have forgotten she was wearing lipstick and now it's in her teeth. "Why don't we talk at lunchtime?"

Oh man. I'm totally going to be interrogated. "Okay."

She nods and heads back to the front. I really need to pee. Sometimes when I get nervous my bladder is like, I have formulated an escape plan, sire, and I'm sure it means well, but it's not that simple. How am I supposed to ask to go to the bathroom now? I would have to raise my hand and draw *more* attention to myself. Mrs. Strachan probably thinks I'm a flight risk anyway.

I chew on the tip of my thumb for a second. Not the nail. The actual thumb. It's uncomfortable enough that I can ignore my bladder.

"Why'd you do it?" a quiet voice asks.

I glance to my right, surprised. *Klieba* is leaning toward me. For a moment, I'm too shocked to reply. He has broken our unspoken bond of silence. For shame, Klieba.

He's even paler than me, with mousy features, small dark eyes, and a bowl cut, and he either grows very slowly or wears hand-me-downs, because his clothes are way too big for him. Even his shoes are, like, three sizes too big. His heels slip out of them as he leans over.

"I didn't," I whisper, feeling my cheeks burning.

"You can tell me." Klieba looks around conspiratorially. "Last year I stole Mr. Carter's right shoelace. He changed into boots for the yard and left them unattended. I still have it, man!"

I frown at him. "I . . . I didn't take the ring."

Klieba grins and puts a finger to his lips like we are now in cahoots or something. "Understood. Meet me outside later if you want to talk. I've been planning my next heist."

What is happening?! I get falsely accused of one felony and now I'm a supervillain?

"His wife is *dead*, you know," another voice says.

Oh no. Not Allison Gaisson. She was suspended in third grade for throwing a plum at Julie. It *exploded*, and for a second, it looked like Julie was dead. I still get nervous whenever Allison eats fruit.

But apart from the exploding-plum incident, she mostly saves the bullying for me. I've never figured out what I did wrong, but my mere existence seems to bother her.

"Yeah," I murmur.

I really have to pee now. My bladder feels like it's the size of an accursed basketball.

"That ring is all he has to remember her by," Allison continues. "You know that, right?"

I'm not sure that's true. They probably took photos and he does have a daughter, but I guess that's irrelevant.

I squeeze my legs together. It actually kind of works, but I don't know why. What if I am squeezing urine into my other organs? What if my stomach is full of pee now? Oh man. Things are deteriorating fast. What if I actually pee my pants? I'm wearing blue jeans, but they're my lightest pair and you would totally see the stain.

"Do you have *anything* to say for yourself?" Allison demands.

"I have to pee!" I shout.

Mrs. Strachan drops her marker. Half the class starts laughing. Klieba is looking around, probably hoping to use the distraction to find something to steal. I need to start watching my backpack. But I have bigger problems now.

I don't even wait for permission. I just hurry out of the class and run for the bathroom.

When I get to the urinal, it's barely a dribble. It was either a false alarm or the pee is sloshing around in my heart.

I turn to my reflection, running my hands down my face. I can't go back there—I've just shouted the word *pee*. I can't go to this school, period. I need to flee the state.

Okay. Just relax, Green. You can stay in here for a while and let things blow over—

A seventh grader walks in, looks at me, and snorts. "I heard you stole Coach's ring."

Never mind. I have to change schools.

I have a new reading spot. My old location was by the portable classroom steps because it was comfortable *and* I could see Cedar playing basketball. It's just sensible to have your bodyguard within eyesight. But now I'm an accused criminal and in hiding, so my new spot is *behind* the portable classroom next to a shrub. Actually, it's just a clump of prickly thistles.

Of course, I'm not totally reckless. I told Cedar where I was in case of any assassination attempts, though I have no idea what his response time would be. I wish I had those ninja stars.

I just finished my "conversation" with Mrs. Strachan, who definitely thinks I stole the ring. She asked me, like, five times and finally just said, "Coach is very upset, Green. You need to think about what you're doing."

It's all because I'm an Asperger kid. No one trusts a butt sandwich. So now I am an exile reading next to a patch of thistles, plotting a possible escape to the Yukon. My life is in shambles.

I hear movement and flinch, ready to throw my book at an assassin. Instead, Cedar plops down beside me, letting his sneakers flop out on the grass next to my Crocs. He looks exhausted.

"Did Coach find his ring?" I ask hopefully.

He shakes his head. "Nope. And he was definitely wearing the ring right before the tryout. Brooks confirmed it. He stopped by Coach's classroom to ask if he could get the balls out and warm up. . . . He arrived at, like, four thirty. Keener.

Anyway, Coach was still wearing the ring in his classroom, grading papers."

"So what are you saying?" I ask.

"I'm saying everyone thinks you took it and are just too embarrassed to admit it. Or . . ."

"Or what?"

Cedar glances at me. "Or that you just don't understand it's wrong."

"Do they think I'm a psychopath—"

"No . . . I don't know. It was Mo who said that last part. We almost got in a fight again. The yard is *tense*."

I feel a strange mixture of emotions. I'm getting better at recognizing them on people's faces, but it's still hard to pick them out in myself sometimes. Or at least to make sense of them. I feel sadness, for sure. That one's easy. It's like someone put a rock in my stomach.

There's anger, too. That one is a sunburn on the inside of your skin and you can't use aloe vera so you have to scream at people instead. I can feel both of those right now, which makes sense.

But there's also . . . embarrassment. Which is weird, because I didn't steal the ring. But there's a mean voice that says, *You didn't take it but you deserve this anyway because you're a weirdo. And now you've humiliated your brother because you couldn't make it through a tryout.*

I'm not used to this feeling. It's pressure behind the eyes. It's a bigger stomach rock.

"I think I want to go home," I murmur.

Cedar shakes his head. "Nah. If you bail out, then they'll definitely think you're guilty."

"What am I going to do, Cedar?"

I'm trying not to cry because I'm supposed to be a ninja but this is a *big rock*.

"Just be patient," Cedar says soothingly. "It will blow over. Or I'll punch Mo in the nose and get suspended." With that, he pulls out his cell phone and starts scrolling through TikTok.

"Are we done planning or . . . ?"

"Huh?" He looks up. "Oh. Yeah. Would you be up for a basketball dance—"

I groan and go back to my book, blinking back any stray tears. "No."

"It'll just be a one-minute routine—"

"*No.*"

I hear movement again and look up. My breath catches in my throat. It's Coach. Immediately I slip my hand into my pocket, gripping the bouncy ball.

"Green, son," he says. His voice is thick. "I've been thinking a lot this morning."

I exchange a worried look with Cedar, who slowly lowers his phone.

"And I don't blame you for being mad," Coach continues. He takes his ball cap off for some reason and holds it in front of him. "But I really need that ring. If you broke the chain or something, no problem. I can buy another one. But I need Renee's ring. Please give it back."

I open my mouth to protest, but Coach holds a hand up to stop me.

"So here's the deal," he says. "No repercussions. Nothing. Classroom door is open like always. I'm going to go to the teachers' lounge after the last bell for a coffee. If the ring is just magically back on my desk, well then, silly me, I must have missed it. No questions asked."

I feel like his eyes are pushing me into the dirt. I can't look at him, but I *feel* his gaze. I can hear the desperation in his voice. But I don't know what to say. I just roll the ball around.

"Coach," Cedar says quietly, "Green doesn't have it."

"Just . . . the door is open," Coach says, keeping his voice steady. "See you boys later."

And then he is gone again, stalking toward the school, and I have to pee. I guess my bladder thinks it can get rid of the rock that way, which sounds like a very bad plan.

Everything keeps getting worse. Coach is sad. Everyone thinks I'm evil. I'm reading next to a clump of *thistles*.

"It'll all blow over soon," Cedar says.

But even he doesn't sound convinced.

CHAPTER 10

CEDAR

I stare at the lone piece of printer paper plastered to the gym double doors with an excessive amount of masking tape. The final roster for the Palmerston Panthers senior basketball team.

It was supposed to be posted at lunch yesterday, but Coach was obviously distracted. It's now Tuesday afternoon, and he finally put it up for last recess.

And there's no Green.

I guess I knew this was coming. He did get thrown out of the tryout. Not to mention accused of stealing a wedding ring. But I wanted to think it would magically turn up this morning and Coach would feel bad and all of my master plans would still come to fruition.

But no. No ring. No vindication.

It's been a total nightmare since that last tryout. Green isn't even at school today. He was so upset when he got home that Mom decided to let him "start the weekend early." I've had two shouting matches with Mo today alone. No matter what I say, everyone is completely convinced Green stole it. Even my best friend.

Well . . . *former* best friend.

I review the names again. The team is pretty much the same as last year, minus Carl Freburg. . . . Brooks Poupore took his spot. Brooks squealed when he saw his name up there.

I can see Mo eyeing me. Actually, most of the guys are. They all knew how badly I wanted Green on the team, so they must be waiting for my reaction.

Brooks clears his throat. "I've been thinking about the three-two zone and—"

"Well?" Corrado says, cutting him off. "Are you going to play or not, Cedar?"

"What?" I ask.

Corrado shifts uncomfortably. "You said you were going to sit out the season. Remember?"

Oh yeah. I forgot about my parting threat.

I probably should sit out. I mean, Coach has now falsely accused my brother *and* cut him from the team. But . . . it's basketball. It's my life. I could try to join an AAU team, but I love playing for the Panthers. Not to mention the AAU tryouts already happened a month ago. If I sit out, I might not be able to play competitive ball for a full *year*. That would put me way behind.

And I'd be miserable. My bedroom is a basketball shrine. I sleep in my ball shorts. My entire life plan is to play in the NBA and be a viral trick-shot star.

"I'm playing," I mutter, trying to sound as gruff and unhappy as possible.

A few of the guys slump in visible relief, but Mo glares at me, his arms crossed. He's wearing a sleeveless jersey today, and he's pushing his arms down against his chest so that it looks like has biceps.

We do that trick all the time at away games. How dare he use it against me.

"What?" I snap at him, folding my arms across my chest too.

I'm wearing sleeves today. Wide ones. Ugh . . . I look totally biceps-less.

"Nothing."

"Say it," I demand.

He hesitates. "Green was never going to make it. But I think I speak for all of us when I say that you need to get that ring back, dude. Coach is messed up. It's going to ruin the season."

The hallway goes quiet. Brooks takes a step back, wide eyes darting between us.

"Green didn't take the ring," I say coldly.

Mo holds my gaze. "So who did, Cedar? Did it disappear into thin air?"

"I don't know."

Without even meaning to, I've taken a step toward him. I can hear the others shifting.

"I heard Coach is thinking about pressing charges," Mo says, pushing his arms down even harder.

His pretend biceps grow larger. I know the truth . . . but it still looks threatening.

"That's the stupidest thing I've ever heard. There're no evidence Green took it."

"Just that the weird kid with assburger was the only one who could have taken it."

I take another step. "I told you there is a *P sound*. And don't call my little brother weird."

"He *is* weird, Cedar."

I stop less than a foot away from his face. Mo is, like, six inches shorter than me, but he has his chin raised, sporadic goatee hairs and all, and we are making some serious eye contact. I can tell he just ate a tuna sandwich with pickles for lunch.

It smells absolutely horrible, but I can't back away now.

"Say it again," I whisper.

"Guys," Brooks says meekly. "We're all on the same team. See, it's right there—"

"Quiet, Brooks," I snap, balling my trembling hands into fists. "Go on, Mo. Say it again."

Mo and I have never had a real fight before. We've barely even argued, other than the rare occasion about Green. We've play-wrestled, though, and I know he's surprisingly strong and totally not against kneeing me in the groin. I'll need to strike fast.

Everything goes still.

"Just get the ring back," Mo says finally, shaking his head and starting down the hallway.

The rest of the team follows him. I can hear my heart pounding in my ears.

Mo is right about one thing: Coach is upset. The team is divided. If we start the season like this, it's going to be a complete disaster. I glance at Coach's open classroom door.

It's time to put an end to this.

• • •

"Great news, bro!"

Green looks up from his book. He's reading in his Star Wars pajamas, despite the fact it's, like, four o'clock. I literally just got home from school. My mom has never let me skip class in my life, and Green gets to hang out in his room and wear pajamas all day. Figures.

I plunk down beside him on the bed, grinning.

"Coach found the ring?" Green says eagerly, placing his book aside.

"No. But we are going to find it for him!"

Green looks at me for a long moment. "I don't get it."

"I had a talk with Coach. He still totally thinks you stole it."

"How is this good news—"

I hold a hand up to stop him. "*But* he agrees that things are getting out of control. You had to stay home from school, he's barely sleeping, I almost got in another fight with Mo today—"

"You did what—"

"Just listen!" I say, leaning forward excitedly. "So I say, 'Coach, let's make a deal. If Green and I find the ring and prove that somebody else took it, then you not only need to apologize to Green, but you have to put him on the team and let him start our first home game!'"

"What?" he whispers.

"This is great news, Green! Here's the key: Coach said he'll cooperate. We can search his classroom and the gym office, we can ask him questions . . . anything we need. Coach still thinks that you have the ring, but he agreed because he 'just wants his ring back.' Do you understand what I'm saying? We can prove you're innocent!"

Green just groans and goes back to his book. "You're crazy."

"We can do this, Green!"

"No."

"So you're just going to give up? Pretend everything will go back to normal?"

He pauses. "I was looking into the Yukon—"

"I need your help, Green. You're a genius. I was just going to be the really cool Watson."

Green lowers his book again. "And what happens if we don't find it? Or if we do find it, but without any evidence of *who* took it? Everyone will just assume that I had it the entire time."

"Well . . . we'll just have to find the evidence. Don't you read the Hardly Boys?"

"*Hardy* Boys," Green corrects, rolling his eyes. "And yes . . . I've read every one of them."

"Well . . . do they ever fail?" I ask.

"It's a book!"

"I need your help, Green," I say, finally catching his eyes. "But I'll go it alone if I have to. I refuse to let everyone at school believe you're a thief. And if I have to search every inch of that school to prove that you didn't take it and they are all stupid jerks, I will."

Green starts to chew on his thumb. Not the nail . . . the actual thumb. I hate it when he does that. "Okay."

"Really?"

"We'll try," he says. "But I don't care about basketball. Honestly. I just want to go back to normal."

I wrap him in a hug. "We'll figure it out, little bro. Now stop squirming and hug me back—"

"Get off!" he manages, laughing as he wriggles free and heads for his bookshelf.

He plucks out one of his many hardcover Hardy Boys books. I catch a glimpse of the cover: two boys staring at something with *The Secret of the Old Mill* written above their heads.

"I say we get started first thing tomorrow morning," I suggest.

Green nods and turns back to me. "Agreed. The Case of the Missing Ring has begun."

CHAPTER 11

GREEN

On Wednesday morning I walk into the second possible crime scene, my footsteps echoing in the empty classroom. Sort of. Crocs are very stealthy.

I look around, feeling strangely uneasy. There's something unsettling about an empty classroom. It's one of those places that is supposed to be full, so when it isn't, it feels wrong.

It's like people. If Cedar is quiet for a day, then something must be wrong. If I am quiet for a day, then I am just Green. It's all about expectations.

Which, I guess, is why everyone assumes I'm the thief. Deep down, they always expected I'd do something wrong.

We've already checked the gym office—it's a tiny, windowless room right outside the gym doors with a desk and some old filing cabinets that every gym teacher and coach shares. Coach swears he left the ring in there the night of the tryout, but our search turned up nothing.

So it was off to Coach's classroom to see if he possibly misplaced it here.

"Let's check the desk first," I suggest.

"You got it, boss," Cedar says, following me in.

As Cedar starts rifling through the drawers, I crouch down behind the desk, looking for any nooks or crannies that a wedding ring could fall into. I run my fingers underneath one of the sliding drawers and almost lose them when Cedar slams it shut.

I look up and scowl at him.

"Sorry," he murmurs. "Should we go over the facts again?"

I explained how the Hardy Boys solved their cases last night, and we watched two episodes of *Veronica Mars* as well. Now we both want to be her instead because she is awesome.

I start crawling along the edge of the wall, figuring it could have been kicked beneath the dusty baseboards. There is a little seam where they meet the tiles . . . a ring might just fit in there.

"Okay," I say. "First thing we know for sure: Coach was wearing his chain *before* the tryout on Friday, September twenty-ninth. That was confirmed by a reliable witness." I pause, glancing back at him. "Is Brooks reliable?"

Cedar seems to consider that. "Yeah. He's a bit much sometimes, but he's a good guy."

"Okay. So Coach claims he took the ring off in the gym office and put it on his desk like usual," I say, running my fingers along the seam.

I almost gag as I pull out a long piece of hair from under the baseboard.

"And we know he wasn't wearing it at the start of tryouts just fifteen minutes later," I say, reluctantly continuing with my sweep. "So if we don't find anything in here, let's assume that the ring really was left on the gym office desk."

Cedar holds up a small black clip. "A bobby pin? Coach doesn't even have hair!"

"Stay focused," I say. "I thought about it last night, and we were probably about forty minutes into the tryout before Coach threw me out. I then grabbed my stuff and left through the side door. I did pass in front of the gym office, of course, but I didn't see anyone."

"Can I just say that you really do sound like a detective. It's kind of freaky."

"I told you . . . I read a lot of crime thrillers."

Cedar plunks down in Coach's chair, stroking his chin thoughtfully. "So we have a forty-minute window where someone stole the ring. We just have to figure out who was in the school."

"Exactly."

By the time I reach the door, I have uncovered five more strands of hair, a piece of chewed bubble gum, a paper clip, and a lot of dust. Brushing my knees off, I stand up, eyeing the handle.

I recall what Coach said: He *never* locks any doors at school and doesn't even keep his keys on him. Who would know that? Was it just a lucky guess?

"Coach is tough, man," Cedar says, holding up a sheet of paper. "He told this kid he has to rewrite the whole essay!"

"Cedar!"

He puts the assignment down and shakes his head. "Nothing, bro. But it was a stretch. I told you . . . Coach turned this place upside down. I wouldn't be surprised if he pulled the tiles up."

"Well, he didn't find the gum," I mutter, wiping my hands on my pants.

Mrs. Strachan walks by the classroom with a coffee, then backs up, staring at me. "Green . . ."

"We . . . have permission," I manage.

She narrows her eyes. I can almost smell the maple syrup and suspicion. "To . . . ?"

"We're searching for the missing ring," Cedar says, jumping to his feet. "Heard any rumors in the staff room, Mrs. Strachan? You guys must gossip in there. . . . And she's gone."

Mrs. Strachan is already storming back toward the staff room . . . probably to report us to Coach. She is being super mean today. Usually if I missed a day she would be like, Welcome back, Green! But today it was all raised eyebrows and not even a "Good morning."

I am so sick of being a felon.

Mom is super angry about everything. She already called the principal and said I was being bullied by students *and* staff, and he apparently said, "Well, that ring is very important to Coach Nelson. . . ." She yelled after that. A lot.

But Mom is not a big fan of the investigation, either. Her exact quote: "That is the most ridiculous thing I have ever heard." Now I'm wondering if she was right.

"This isn't going well," I say, looking at my poor fingers.

They touched some unspeakable things this morning. Someone had left an apple core behind the desk in the gym office . . . it had looked and felt like old leather.

"This was just step two, bro," Cedar says consolingly. "Now we move on to witnesses."

I frown. "There were no witnesses."

"Not true," Cedar says, jumping to his feet. "Meet me next recess . . . at Maggie's office. She's the only other person we *know* was in the school. She must have seen something unusual, right?"

"I'm kind of afraid of Maggie," I say.

"Oh, she's terrifying. But she's the key witness."

I follow him toward the yard. "Didn't you tell me she hit a kid with a wet mop?"

"That was probably a rumor." Cedar pauses. "But be ready to run . . . just in case."

When the class files in after the morning bell, Mrs. Strachan is waiting by the whiteboard. She gives me a suspicious look, but I'm guessing Coach confirmed our story because she doesn't arrest me.

I take my seat, frowning as Allison takes the long way to her desk so she can glare at me and mouth, "Give it back." She's either really invested in Coach's missing ring, or she's just enjoying the excuse to bully me now that I have been shunned by society.

I realize I don't know much about Allison. Or Klieba. Or, well, anyone in my class. I kind of just hang out in my own little world and don't really think about my classmates. I guess I'm self-absorbed, but in a completely non-confident way.

I wonder if that has a different name?

"We will be having a math quiz on Friday," Mrs. Strachan says over the scraping of chairs and the shuffling of pencils and Brian Donnelly's sniffling nose. "It will cover everything we've learned in chapter ten. We'll do a little review now. I know some of you have had a tough time with algebra, so make sure you ask plenty of questions."

She doesn't mean me, of course. I've always been good at math. I'm pretty good in school, period, though I got a *Satisfactory* in gym class on my last report card and an even more dreaded *Needs Improvement* in drama.

Dr. Lee warned Mom and Dad that I would never do well in school. He said I was very smart, but that my "lack of social skills might hold me back." Apparently it would be hard for me to find a job one day or have a family for the same reasons. I heard Mom telling her friend Liz about it last year, and she was almost crying.

But honestly, I think I'm doing pretty good. I remember things easily. I can picture numbers in my brain like I am writing them out. Cedar says I'm the smartest kid he's ever met, and he knows me way better than any doctor.

I probably won't be an actor. But I can do lots of other things.

Mrs. Strachan assigns a work period to review the last chapter, but I space out pretty quickly and stare out the window again. Another V formation of geese flies overhead. The leader drops back, letting another goose take the toughest spot, and my mind wanders back to the ring. It's the motive that's puzzling me. Who had a reason to steal the ring?

Was it simply someone who wanted to sell it? It *is* a diamond ring . . . maybe they took it to a pawn shop? I need to discuss the possibility with Cedar.

"You know . . . Lin told me Coach was crying in his car the other day," Allison whispers behind me.

I still can't believe Mrs. Strachan put that plum-throwing menace behind me.

I watch the geese vanish into the wispy clouds, trying to ignore her. I sincerely doubt Coach was actually crying in his car, but Cedar says he really is moody. Apparently he yelled at a pigeon on recess duty this morning. And sure, they poop on stuff, but it's not really their fault.

"I also heard you're holding the ring hostage to use it against Coach one day," she says.

I glance back at her incredulously. She has these really intense green eyes—I wouldn't be surprised if she could shoot lasers out of them—with bright red hair that's always pulled back into a tight ponytail, and thin, really freckly lips that only seem to know how to sneer.

Strangely, Allison seems alarmed when I turn around, and her eyes quickly go to her open backpack on the floor beside her.

I follow her gaze, frowning, but I don't see anything other than a few notebooks poking out.

"What are you looking at?" Allison says, snapping the bag up into her lap.

I flush and turn around again. My bladder prepares an escape plan. And I can't risk diverting the pee again.

"But me?" Allison says. I hear her moving closer. "I think you just threw it in the sewer."

That's both oddly specific and even more insulting than the hostage plan, and I'm about to run to the bathroom when the bell rings anyway, putting an end to Allison's accusations.

Everyone streams out and turns left down the hallway toward the yard. I reluctantly shuffle the other way toward Maggie's janitorial office, wondering if Cedar and I are about to get mopped.

"I don't have time for this," Maggie snaps.

Maggie is a very big lady. Cedar told me she was a former rugby star, and I believe it—she has more muscles than Coach. She's probably about fifty with strands of gray creeping into her curly brown hair and the most impressive frown lines I've ever seen. They're like canyons.

She's the school janitor, groundskeeper, handywoman, and security guard all in one. If someone really did break into the school that night to steal Coach's ring, they're lucky Maggie didn't catch them. She could probably twist my dad into a pretzel.

"Just one minute of your time?" Cedar says, trying his friendliest smile. He has a dimple, and that strange divot in his face seems to be an effective tool. "We have a couple of questions."

She glares at him. "That smile will not work on me, son. I will wipe it right off."

My eyes go to the tin bucket beside her. The water is

murky . . . there could be *bathroom floor* residue in there. She might have just mopped around the urinals. I shudder.

"Please," Cedar says. "Just a few quick questions?"

Maggie grunts and gestures for him to continue.

"Did you see anyone after the final bell on the night of the ring theft?" Cedar asks.

"I saw lots of people," she snaps. "All of them adding to my never-ending work. Boys traipsing around for some ridiculous late-night tryout, for one. Coach asking if *I* vacuumed up his ring, like I'm some sort of idiot. I almost smacked that loud-mouth, but he was too upset."

She eyes me, and I quickly turn my attention to the janitor's cart, flushing.

"I hear you took it, Green," Maggie says quietly. "Is that true?"

I shake my head, slipping my hand into my pocket to find the bouncy ball. My fingers wrap around the smooth rubber, and I roll it around, trying to breathe.

I really don't want to be mopped.

"That's why we're investigating," Cedar says. "To clear his name."

She snorts. "Investigating? What are you boys . . . nine years old?"

"I'm thirteen," Cedar grumbles. "So, you saw no one else between five and six p.m.?"

"How in the world am I supposed to know what time it was? I was busy cleaning up footprints by the side door . . . *after* I had already cleaned that hall! I figured all the students were gone and you boys were in the gym so I could start there, but no. I come back ten minutes later and someone trekked mud in again."

I perk up at that one. I left through the side door that night and stepped in mud just outside. It's not fully paved on that side of the school, and it had rained a lot that day. I remember it vividly because some of the mud seeped into my Crocs.

But I didn't go back inside.

Cedar sighs. "Well, thanks anyway, Maggie."

"I hope you figure out who stole it, boys."

I look up at her. "You . . . believe me?"

"Of course I do," she says. "You just told me you're innocent, didn't you? And I didn't think it sounded like you in the first place. I always thought you were a good kid."

Cedar and I exchange a surprised look. I didn't think anyone had a soft spot for me. Well, Mom and Dad and Cedar. Oma too, but she passed away. Maybe Opa.

"You did?" Cedar asks, frowning.

"Of course. He's my favorite type of kid: quiet, clean, and never running in the hallway." She shoots me a thoughtful look. "You know . . . there's a security camera by the front door. We used to have one at the side door too, but it broke, like, fifteen years ago and no one ever bothered to replace it. But the front one still works. It looks out over the walkway and the parking lot, so if anyone drove up or came in that way, it would be on there. I doubt someone came into the school and took the ring, but it might be worth checking. I told Coach about it, but he just said he already knew who took it so what was the point." She shrugs. "I haven't actually looked at any of the footage in years—I never had a reason—but it does record onto my old computer."

I feel my mouth hanging open. I've seen that security camera before, but I always assumed it was broken . . . it looks like it's a hundred years old.

"That would be awesome!" Cedar says. "Thank you, Maggie!"

She gives us a toothy grin. "I'll find the clip later. You can watch it tomorrow morning. Just come by my office at first recess."

We both hurry down the hallway.

"Well, she is way nicer than I thought," Cedar says. "And she's going to give us a big clue!"

"A second clue," I say, glancing back at Maggie. "She already gave us one."

"What?"

"Maggie said she cleaned that side hallway after the tryout started . . . and then had to do it again because of some muddy footprints. That means someone came in the side door *during* our tryout. I think someone came back to steal the ring."

"Someone who knew we had tryouts," Cedar murmurs.

"Exactly," I say, feeling my excitement growing. "Someone planned a heist, Cedar."

He whistles. "This is getting real, little bro. What do we do now?"

"We'll watch the surveillance footage tomorrow and see if it caught anything. But in the meantime, we start a list of suspects."

CHAPTER 12

CEDAR

Our roof is higher than I thought. Now that I'm up here, our two-story house feels like a skyscraper.

It wasn't easy getting up here, either. I had to climb out of my bedroom window onto the garage and then scramble onto the main roof from there. I'm pretty sure I broke a gutter on the way. Dad is going to kill me if he finds out. . . . That man despises home repairs.

But I made it, and I have my phone and my basketball and a clear shot at the hoop in the driveway. Of course, if I fall off I'm totally going to die, but it's worth it.

It's just before dinnertime, so my suburban street is still fairly busy—people coming home from work, a few kids playing outside, a couple of joggers. But nobody seems to have noticed me yet.

In terms of my household, I picked my time very strategically. Dad goes to the gym at five and Mom starts dinner, so they're both occupied. Green would definitely not approve of this plan either, but he gets his treasured hour of video games at five, so he's out of the picture too.

I take a deep breath and start an Instagram Live.

I'm not going to get a lot of shots at this. Actually . . . probably just one. It was a treacherous climb, and if Mom or Dad sees me up here I'm definitely going to get grounded.

I need to make this count.

My face pops onto the screen—I re-gelled my hair, obviously, and I have a filter on to moderate that zit.

"What up, people," I say. "It's your boy Cedar Bennett attempting the ever-dangerous rooftop three-pointer. Taking bets now: Who thinks I can swish this on the first attempt?"

The comments start to pop up immediately, along with some likes and a few angry faces.

Meghan Hayes: CEDAR BE CAREFUL

Brooks Poupore: You got this man first shot let's go Panthers whoop whoop

Corrado Francis: make it raiiiiiiin Tree

Cherene Sanker: No chance you make it

Jackie Scott: I am going to call your mother

Ugh, why have I not blocked my aunt? I better hurry up.

"Okay, going to make this quick," I say. "Here's the target."

I turn the phone's camera toward the hoop far below on my driveway. My mom's car is parked about ten feet away from it. I did consider the risk, but it's a basketball. . . . Even if I hit the thing, it's not going to matter. Besides, I need to think positive. I am totally going to make this.

I flip the camera back to me for a quick thumbs-up.

"Well, here goes," I say, pointing the view at the hoop again. I have to shoot with one hand, which is *really* not ideal, but I steady the phone with my left hand and raise the ball with my right. "For the win. Three . . . two . . . one!"

I let it fly. For a second, I think it has a chance.

And then it keeps flying . . . past the hoop and straight toward my mom's windshield.

The ball hits the windshield and *impacts*. Half the ball plunges through the glass, and it just lodges itself there, forming pretty undeniable evidence about who and what did the damage.

"Oh no," I murmur.

I hear my front door fly open, and Mom runs onto the driveway, staring at her car.

"Cedar!"

"This is the last straw, Cedar."

I feel like I'm at a tribunal. I'm sitting alone on the couch while Mom paces back and forth across the living room. Dad and Green are peeking out from the kitchen like a legit peanut gallery, probably wondering if it's going to be exile or straight-up execution by death stare.

"I didn't mean—" I start again.

She holds a hand up. "It's gone too far. These ridiculous videos. The cell phone attached to your hand twenty-four seven. Sometimes I feel like there's a zombie walking around the house."

Her eyes flash to my cell phone, which I'm cradling protectively in my lap. Why did I bring the smoking gun to my own trial? Why did I come down from the roof, period? I should have just stayed up there forever. It would be cold at night, but maybe if I huddled by the chimney . . .

"I'm taking your phone for a week," she announces.

I open my mouth, close it again, and then sputter, "What?"

"A full week starting now. Hand it over."

I turn to Dad for support. He looks away. Green is chewing on his thumb. *He* knows what's happening here. Mom isn't just taking my phone.

She is taking my life away for a week.

"You can't," I whisper. "I'll save up for a new windshield. I'll—"

"I don't care about the windshield," she snaps. "Well . . . I do, but I care more about the fact that my son was standing on the *roof* for a stupid social media post."

I grip my phone with both hands, trying a smile. "Mom, let's be reasonable—"

"Give me the phone."

"This is like Gandalf and Bilbo in *The Lord of the Rings*," Green whispers to Dad.

He's been rewatching the series all week.

I reluctantly hand over the phone. She turns it off immediately, and I hear a last ping of a message before it plunges into darkness. Who was it? Mo? Meghan? Keesha revealing that she likes destructive vandals and will date me if I reply in the next hour? My stomach curdles.

I downloaded the video and uploaded it to TikTok out of desperation before I came off the roof, but it was probably a waste of time. I missed the shot so badly I got grounded.

I'm never going to go viral.

"I need my phone," I plead. "Green and I are using it for research."

That's a bit of a stretch, but I am keeping our list of suspects in the Notes app and we did watch an episode of *Veronica Mars* on there, so it's kind of true. But Mom's scowl just deepens.

"For your 'investigation'?" she snaps. "The one that I specifically forbade?"

"I'm trying to clear Green's name, Mom!"

"You're not detectives! You're just going to cause more trouble. Coach is being ridiculous, and he'll realize it soon," she says. "Now go to your room. I'll call you for dinner."

"Don't bother," I shout, jumping to my feet.

She rolls her eyes. "So you're going to starve to death?"

"It's called a hunger strike," I reply. "Look it up."

"Maybe we can play PlayStation instead—" Green volunteers.

"Shut up, Green!" I snap.

It's louder and sharper than I intended, and Green's face goes bright red.

Dad frowns. "Chill out, Cedar."

But I'm in a full-out rage now. I haven't had one of these since I dropped my phone in Corrado's pool and couldn't get a replacement for three days. Three days! Now I'm supposed to make it a week?!

I storm upstairs, flop onto my bed, and stare at the ceiling because what else can I do? I have geography homework, but this is prescheduled *phone time*. I have a social media presence to maintain. A week away could cost me some serious followers. Easily five or six.

I feel a growing pressure behind my eyes, which catches even me off guard. But yeah, you know what . . . I feel like crying.

There's a stream of thoughts going through my head about what I am missing and how unfair this is and how am I ever going to make it a full week without my Spotify—my life will have no soundtrack—and . . . yeah. I am *crying*. Hot tears. Possibly snot.

This would be a super time to call Mo so he could cheer me up like he always does, and we do have a home phone I could use . . . but I can't call him. We're still fighting. I am officially disconnected from the world.

I lie in bed for the rest of the night, ignoring everyone, and fall asleep hungry.

CHAPTER 13

GREEN

"Morning," Cedar grumbles as he stalks into the kitchen, his hair standing on end.

I don't say anything. Cedar doesn't get mad at me often, and he's never told me to *shut up*. Does he never want me to talk to him again? Is there a set time frame? A week or two is doable, but I think a month would be tricky.

I decide to ignore him and get back to work. I dust a few sandwich crumbs off my scattered paperwork and examine my notes.

Breakfast is the time when cheese sandwiches are most vulnerable. There are so many sugary options for breakfast. Once I actually tried a bowl of Lucky Charms, and it was going well for a minute. Then I bit into one of the marshmallows and it was crunchy but also rubbery, somehow. I think it *squeaked* when I ate it. I couldn't figure out what it was made of, so I had to throw out the whole bowl.

But I have considered pancakes, of course, and Cedar was eating a toaster strudel yesterday. He got to put his own icing on! The challenge of maximizing the surface area really appeals to me.

Sure enough, Cedar sits down with two more toaster stru-
dels. I watch as he just dumps the packet of icing into a single
blob. Ugh. What a waste.

"What are you doing?" he asks, eyeing my paperwork.

I hesitate. Does this mean Uno-reverse shut up? "Umm . . .
investigating."

He takes a sullen bite out of a strudel. It looks so flaky. No.
It's not worth the risk. There is some sort of fruit filling in
there. It could have seeds. Imagine a raspberry seed stuck in
your teeth . . . *forever*? No thank you.

"Is that a map of the school?" Cedar asks, tilting his head to
get a better look.

I grin and spin the hand-drawn map toward him. It took me
a full hour last night.

"I highlighted the important spots: the side door, the gym
office, Coach's classroom, and the staff room."

Cedar frowns. "The staff room?"

"There may still have been teachers in the school during tryouts. Teachers always stay after school to clean up and do some
grading. They have to be suspects too."

"How are we going to investigate teachers?" Cedar asks
through another bite of strudel.

"We just need to find motives. You'll need to interview
Coach soon. I've split the suspects into three separate categories:
teachers, students, and outsiders. Here . . . take a look."

I pass him the chart. It was the crowning achievement of my
evening.

STUDENTS
Brooks
Andrew Staff
Corrado
Jerome
Carl Freburg
Guy with the red
shoes*
*ask Cedar
Mo
Brad Something
Everyone else who
tried out—I don't
remember their
names
All the other students
in our school

TEACHERS
Mrs. Strachan
Mrs. Clark
Mr. Consoli
Mr. Pryor
Mrs. Slater
Ms. Kumentas
The teacher who
wears suits
Mr . . . Suit?
Principal Nickel
Ask Cedar for
more teacher
names

OUTSIDERS
Burglar
Mafia Connection
Zombie Wife
Coach is
delusional and
stole it himself
Ringwraiths

Cedar sighs, tosses his half-eaten strudel on the plate, and takes my chart. "Even ignoring the ridiculous Outsiders column, I have a lot of questions. But honestly, Green . . . a zombie wife?"

"I was just covering all our bases," I murmur.

"Okay, A . . . why is Brooks the number-one suspect for students? He was with us, remember? B, the dude with the red shoes is Lee; you've met him a hundred times. C, Mr. Suit? Really?"

"What's his name again?" I ask, getting my pen ready.

"Mr. Rodrigues. And *no*, I won't tell you any more teacher names. There is no way it was a teacher, dude."

I cross my arms, feeling a bit pouty. I worked hard on that chart. "You never know."

"Give me the pen. I'm going to start crossing some out."

"We didn't do our due diligence yet!"

He snatches the marker, glaring at me. "I think we can remove ringwraiths."

I pause, then nod. "That was just wishful thinking."

Cedar goes through the chart, crossing out an awful lot of options. He is obviously still angry about the phone. His mouth is set in a line and he's crossing things out so hard his hand is shaking. I hope he doesn't break my marker.

Finally, he throws it down and sits back, rubbing his hands across his face like Mom does when she puts on moisturizer. When he looks up, his green eyes are bloodshot from all the rubbing.

Without thinking, I slide my chair back, alarmed.

"Do you know where my phone is?" he asks.

"No. Mom hid it somewhere."

"*Where?*" he says. He's almost shouting. Between that and the red eyes, I'm kind of freaked out. He went from Bilbo to Gollum in a single night.

"I don't know!" I say. "She didn't tell me."

"This is ridiculous. A full week because of a stupid windshield?"

I slowly slide my chart back across the table. "Dad said it would cost five hundred dollars."

"They have insurance," he mutters. "I barely slept last night. I woke up and it was like I literally couldn't do anything to relax. I tried to count sheep, but I don't even know what the point of that is. Are they standing in a herd? Or are they just walking by me going, Baa, Cedar?"

I *was* inspecting the crossed-out names, but I look up, concerned. "Are you crazy now?"

"It's like she cut my arm off, bro. You know what I mean?"

I look down at my arm, frowning. "No . . . ?"

"I feel so isolated. I have no idea what anyone is doing. It's brutal."

"You know what I'm doing."

He groans. "I mean my friends. They could be having a party right now for all I know."

"Are there parties in the morning?" I ask curiously.

"Ugh. Never mind."

I check the time on the stove and start packing up my notes. It's already eight fifteen, and I still have thirty-two teeth to brush. Sleuthing is no excuse for poor hygiene.

"I don't have a phone," I say, shrugging as I stack the papers. "I don't mind."

"Well, I don't know how you do it. How do you keep in touch with friends . . . ?" Cedar pauses, clearly trying to think of a more suitable approach. "Okay, how do you get news?"

"Mom."

"How do you get directions?"

"I only go to school and back."

Cedar rubs his forehead again, groaning. "Okay, never mind the practical stuff. It's also the *possibilities* of my phone. Like what if Tom Holland just followed me on Instagram and was like, Hey dude, love the content, want to come hang out today? Wouldn't that be so awesome?"

"Is he Spider-Man or Tom Holland? I don't know Tom Holland, so I would have to pass."

"You don't know Spider-Man, either!" he shouts.

"Yeah, but he might give me a web blaster or discover super-powers in me or something, so I'd take the chance." I start upstairs, tucking my notes into my backpack on the way.

Cedar plops his head down on the table with a thud. "You're impossible."

"You better get ready," I say, leaning over the banister . . . just slightly. I'm not reckless. "We have a busy day of investigations. For all we know, Maggie has already found the culprit!"

Maggie is sitting in her office when we arrive during first recess . . . eating a cheese sandwich. Wow, I *really* misjudged her. Maggie is my new favorite person in the entire school.

"Boys," she says, giving us a curt nod. "Come in."

We enter the small office. It's basically just a desk, a computer, a mini fridge, and a bunch of buckets and mops and tools and stuff. I've heard that Maggie can fix anything. She even fixes the teachers' cars in the parking lots.

The more I think about it, the more I wonder where her "scary" reputation comes from. Was it just the one mopping? It doesn't seem *that* bad. Well, it all depends on the previous mopping spot. I've seen the floor beneath those urinals.

"Well?" Cedar asks eagerly, positioning himself in front of the computer.

"Got the video," Maggie says. "But it's not much."

She pulls up a file on her computer and clicks play. The video is extremely grainy. It's not black-and-white, but the colors are very muted, like it's covered in a layer of dust or dirt.

The camera shows the walkway, aiming outward from its spot on the exterior wall just above the front doors. The parking lot is also in view at the top of the frame, and as Maggie fast-forwards the video, I can see students and teachers exiting the school. It looks like they're moving around in a sandstorm.

"How old is this camera?" Cedar grumbles.

Maggie snorts. "Old. But see the time down there?"

I check the bottom left corner of the video, where a string of small white numbers lists the date and time. It's from Friday the twenty-eighth at five thirty-six p.m. I frown. That's almost when I left.

"Watched it myself last night," Maggie says, taking a sip of water and leaning forward to check the time. "Ms. Kumentas left through the front door around five thirty. I already fast-forwarded the video before you came. . . . It looks like she was the last teacher to leave that night. You can see her get into her car and drive away, and then . . . there! Did you see it?"

"No," Cedar says, frowning.

I did. In the top right corner of the video, at the very edge of the parking lot, a bicycle streaked by.

It was only the bottom part of the bike . . . just some tires and pumping sneakers, but it was headed *away* from the school. And fast.

It doesn't necessarily mean anything. It could have just been a cyclist on a shortcut through the school parking lot . . . but that would be a pretty weird shortcut. I dig my hand-drawn map out of my pocket and think about the direction the bike was heading. *If* they were leaving out the side door with a stolen ring in their pocket, that would be the way to do it. It's a definite lead.

"The thief might have been on that bike," I murmur.

Maggie nods, though Cedar is still looking between us, confused. "What bike?"

"What do you got there?" Maggie asks, and I hand over the map. She smirks. "Just like a real detective."

"Show her the suspect page," Cedar mutters.

Her eyes light up. "Let's see it! I have to admit . . . I kind of like all this investigating business. I wanted to be a police officer once upon a time. Still could, I suppose. I'm getting tired of all these kids messing up my hallways." She pauses. "No offense."

"None taken," I assure her, passing over the suspect list.

She looks that over and chuckles. "Zombie wife . . . that's a good one."

I glance at Cedar, who rolls his eyes.

"I'm surprised you don't have the vice principal on here," Maggie says, handing it back. "To be clear, I sincerely doubt a teacher took it, but she's far more likely than Mr. Consoli."

"Mrs. Frost?" Cedar asks. "Why?"

"Because Mrs. Frost and Coach do *not* get along. She thinks he's a nutcase. He thinks she's . . . well, words that shouldn't be repeated. They are archenemies. But again, it's a stretch."

"I'll add her name anyway," I say quickly. "Thank you."

"Ms. Sanders, too . . . ," Maggie says thoughtfully through another bite. "She's been avoiding Coach in the staff room for a month or two now. Maybe they got into an argument?"

Cedar frowns. "How do you know all this?"

"I enjoy some teacher drama," she says, shrugging. "Keeps my day interesting."

I, of course, am already scribbling both names onto my suspect list.

"It's weird," Maggie continues. "I could have sworn I locked that side door. I always do. But it was unlocked when I checked that night. The one day I forget, someone comes in." She scowls and cracks her knuckles. "If I ever catch someone sneaking around after hours, there will be repercussions."

I think about that, frowning. It seems like a *very* unfortunate coincidence.

Cedar starts backing out of the office. "Right. Well . . . thanks, Maggie."

"Go get 'em, boys. Green, if anyone bothers you, let me know. I'll sort it out."

Awesome! I have a new lead and an official bodyguard now. Things are really looking up.

"Thanks, Maggie," I say, then rush after Cedar.

I tug on his arm, grinning. "We have a getaway vehicle. The culprit has a bike. I think it was red."

"How could you tell?"

I tuck the map and chart back into my pocket. "It looked reddish brown, but you don't see a lot of reddish-brown bikes. I think that was the camera."

"Does that mean we can officially eliminate the staff?" Cedar asks. "Since, you know, they have cars."

"Not yet. You need to ask Coach about Mrs. Frost. . . . She could have hired a thief."

He glances at me, raising his eyebrows. "Why?"

"To get Coach fired! She probably knew he would get angry and do something bad."

Cedar groans. "Dude, it was clearly a student. Or just a straight-up thief who decided to rob the school. They do exist, you know."

"I thought of that, actually. We need to look into local pawn shops. Isn't there one a few blocks from the school?"

"Yeah . . . Promotion Pawn. I got a cheap acoustic guitar from there once. I thought I could make some singing videos." He sighs. "I overlooked the fact that I can't play guitar. Or sing."

"I remember," I say, making a face. It wasn't a great week for reading. "Well, let's go check it out soon. Also, will you schedule that interview with Coach? I can't be there, obviously. His fingers look very strangle-y when he sees me. "

"Fine." Cedar stops and turns to me, digging his hands into his pockets. "And . . . sorry about yesterday," he murmurs. "I was upset."

"It's okay."

He shakes his head. "No, it's not. I just got a little pressed and said stuff I didn't mean. Don't ever shut up on my account. That's exactly what I *don't* want from you. Do the opposite."

"Open down?"

"What? No. Just . . . I'm sorry. I know you're still getting a hard time around here. We're going to find the thief and arrest them, okay? Or, you know, call Maggie to beat them up. It's going to get better soon." I nod, and he shoots me a lopsided grin. "We're still a team, then?"

"Still a team," I confirm.

"Good. Come on . . . I need to blow off some steam before my Coach interview."

"Think he'll cooperate?" I ask hopefully, following him toward the yard.

Cedar pauses. "No."

CHaPTeR 14

CEDAR

Coach plops onto his chair and immediately starts tapping his index finger on the desk. We're meeting in the gym office. . . . Green and I have both decided that this is likely the official crime scene, as Coach claimed. Someone came into this tiny office and stole Coach's ring.

Now we just have to figure out who. And why, I guess. And possibly how. Ugh.

Coach's unblinking eyes land on me and I fidget. He really is edgy lately. That pigeon never came back.

I open my notebook, which Green insisted I bring along. He said it gave me a "more professional appearance." He also wrote down a few questions he wanted me to ask, though I refuse to ask Coach if he has undergone a psychiatric evaluation lately or if he owes anyone money . . . specifically the Mafia. We have our first practice tonight after school and I really don't want to run wind sprints the entire time.

I start with Green's first question. "Did you call the police?"

"Yes," he grunts. "And I even told them I knew who stole it."

"Coach!"

He waves a hand in dismissal. "They said they couldn't do

anything without proof. All they did was file a stolen item report in case it turns up."

I make a note of that, thankful the police didn't show up at my door. I can't imagine Green having to answer questions from a *police officer*. "Are you sure this door was unlocked?"

He nods. "Yes. Like I said, I never lock this door. I got locked out once by another teacher, and it was *very* annoying. In fact, this year all of the coaches and gym teachers decided there was nothing in this office to steal, and that we wouldn't lock it anymore."

I write down a *Yes* beside the question and move on to the next one.

"Okay. Now, would you say it's common knowledge you leave the ring in here during practice? I know you told the team, but does anyone else know? Staff? Friends? Loan sharks?"

I cough, trying to cover up that last part.

Coach rolls his eyes. "I don't use loan sharks. And yes, I guess everyone knows that. I mean, I don't go around announcing it, but I think most people heard about last year's . . . incident when I lost the ring in the Pringle Creek gym. It caused a bit of a stir."

I write down another *Yes* beside that question.

"And is it true you never take the ring off otherwise? For example—" I clear my throat. "While making coffee in the staff room. While peeing. While doing laundry. While changing tires on a car. While shaving your—"

"*No,*" Coach cuts in, his face reddening. "I don't take it off otherwise. Abby did say I shouldn't be wearing it all the time—I think she's afraid I'll lose it somewhere else. . . . I get angry watching football sometimes—but I just prefer to keep it close."

I look up. "Does Abby still hang out with Keesha Adams, by chance?"

Coach frowns. "I think so. Why?"

"No reason," I say, pen pausing over the paper. "Do you ever think about hosting a team party? But also letting Abby host a party at the same time? Might as well combine them, right? What about next Friday . . . ?"

"What are you talking about?" Coach demands. "I'm trying to get Abby to do a little less partying these days, thank you. And are you trying to flirt with my daughter? She's a bit old for you, son."

"Don't I know it," I say mournfully. I make a note: *Always wears it.* "Do you have any enemies among the staff?"

"What?" he sputters.

"Is it true you don't get along with Mrs. Frost? What about Ms. Sanders?"

Coach has this squiggly vein in his forehead that bulges sometimes—usually when Mo says something hilarious—and it is *bulging.* It looks like a python eating another python.

"What does that have to do with anything?" Coach snaps. "And why do you mention those names? What have you heard? Did Layne say something? I better talk to her. Are there rumors in the schoolyard? And sure, Mrs. Frost and I have had our disagreements, but . . . Don't write that down!"

I make a note that Coach definitely doesn't get along with Mrs. Frost. I also write down *Layne* because I'm not sure who that is.

"Just covering all our bases," I murmur.

Coach rubs his eyeballs with his palms. It looks painful. "This is ridiculous."

"Two more questions. Number one: Have you yelled at anyone besides Green lately?"

"We're done here," Coach says. "I have things to do. I'll see you at practice tonight."

"Can I search the gym again after practice?" I ask.

"No! I have plans later—" He scowls. "Why am I explaining myself? You are not a detective, Cedar. I shouldn't have agreed to this. Besides, I've searched the gym. See you later."

I make a note of *Probably yelled at someone.* Then I start for the door, my pen still hovering over the page. "Final question: Who was the last person to leave the gym on Wednesday after the tryouts?"

Coach frowns. "I was. I cleaned up."

"So the rest of the players trying out left before you. Like . . . all twenty of them?"

"Only by a minute or two," he says, clearly guessing where I'm going with this. "And they were in a group."

"How do you know?"

Coach hesitates. "Well . . . they all walked out of the gym together."

I make a note and smile. That felt like a courtroom drama where I just scored a last point interviewing the witness. Hear that, jury? There were *twenty other kids* in the school that night.

"Thank you, Coach."

"I know Green took it," Coach says quietly. "I saw the look in his eyes."

I turn back to him. "First of all, that's a lie. Green doesn't even make eye contact with adults. You're just saying that because you think Green is different. It's the same reason everyone else in this stupid school thinks he stole it. And I can't wait to prove you all wrong."

"Well, I hope you do," Coach grumbles. "I just want my ring back."

"And remember our deal: Green starts the first game when we prove his innocence."

"*If* you prove it, then a deal is a deal."

I nod and hurry down the hallway. I don't think I got much evidence, but I'll let Green be the judge of that. What I did get from the interview was another jolt of motivation. I'm so sick of everyone assuming Green took it. It's like they won't even consider the possibility he's innocent.

And that's a problem. Because if we don't solve the mystery, Green is guilty by default. Forever. And all my plans for him playing basketball and making new friends go down the drain.

It means there really is no alternative here. We *have* to find that ring.

CHapter 15

GREEN

"Why have I never been here before?" I whisper to Cedar, looking around with wide eyes.

It's Friday evening—exactly one week since the ring's disappearance—and we've finally made it to Promotion Pawn. And it is awesome. It has old video games, flat-screen TVs, musical instruments, a bunch of swords for some reason . . . it legitimately has it all. Including jewelry.

"Stay focused," Cedar says, eyeing a huge glass case full of necklaces and rings. "Any of these look familiar?"

I reluctantly turn away from the swords, studying the rows of jewelry. "I don't think so. But it's hard to be sure. I only looked at the ring closely once. It had a pretty big diamond on it."

"Yeah . . . I don't think it's here either. Let's go talk to the cashier."

We slowly move toward the front counter, where a wiry, middle-aged bald man with round glasses looks up from a book. I quickly avert my eyes, but not before I see him scowl.

He's wearing a name tag with *Peter* written very neatly in black marker.

"Yes . . . *children?*" he says. Peter doesn't sound friendly.

Cedar casually leans against the counter, drumming the surface with his fingers. We've been watching a lot of detective shows. "Question for you, Peter: Has anyone tried to sell you a ring recently?"

"People try to sell me lots of things," Peter replies coolly. "Why?"

"It was stolen from our . . . father," Cedar says. "More personal," he whispers to me.

I risk a glance as Peter lowers the book. He looks like a mean, bald owl. Wearing a tuxedo T-shirt. So maybe a mean, bald penguin. "I see. And I presume I'm to just turn over my receipts to you? Play back my security footage? Reveal every seller in our history?"

"That would be super," Cedar agrees.

"No. I don't deal with criminals anyway. Except for the one case with that saxophone."

Cedar and I look at each other, frowning. I gesture with my chin toward the door. Swords or not, I don't like Promotion Pawn after all. It has mean clerks and possibly stolen saxophones.

"Why doesn't he talk?" Peter said, and I can feel his eyes on me.

"He's a . . . mime," Cedar says. Boy, he's just lying for fun now. "Are you sure there wasn't anyone selling a ring—"

"There was a kid here yesterday with a ring," another louder voice cuts in. "And you are officially relieved, Peter Pan. It's four thirty."

I look up and see a bearded man come out of the back room,

drinking an absolutely enormous soda. He has Cheetos crumbs in his beard and *Fergus* scrawled in barely legible pen across his name tag.

Peter glares at him. "A, I despise that nickname. B, we don't need to—"

"That kid had lots of stuff to sell," Fergus cuts in, completely ignoring his coworker and plopping onto a chair. Peter just throws his hands up and heads for the back room. "He even tried to sell me an alarm clock. I was like, 'Kid, people have phones these days.'"

"What did he look like?" Cedar asks quickly.

Fergus shrugs. "I don't know. Brown hair. Probably brown eyes. I presume a nose."

"Very descriptive," Cedar mutters. "Well . . . did you buy the ring?"

"Nah," Fergus says. "I mean, I would have taken it, but he wanted more money. Said he needed the cash for something. I told him to come back with more stuff and maybe we could talk. He's supposed to come back today." He peers at us. "Probably about your age, actually. Weird."

"Not really," Cedar says, giving me a meaningful look. "Do you know what time he was coming back? Or maybe when he was here yesterday?"

"I don't know, dude . . . six maybe? Maybe five. What time is it now?" He chuckles and scratches his beard. "Probably should have bought that alarm clock."

"Thanks," Cedar says, then pulls my arm and leads me out of the store.

"Where are we going?" I ask as soon as the door shuts behind us.

"To set up a stakeout, obviously. The ring thief could be here at any moment."

"Mom is going to be so mad," I say, nervously checking the time on my watch: five forty.

We had told Mom and Dad that we were going to the park to toss the bouncy ball around—a poor excuse, really . . . our bumpy driveway is an amazing bouncy ball arena—but they seemed to buy the story. Still, we'd only had an hour and a half before dinner, at most.

We'd been staking out the pawn shop for nearly an hour now, and there was no way we would be home in time.

"She'll be fine," Cedar says, popping another ketchup chip in his mouth. His lips are already bright red. "It will all be worth it when we crack this case open."

Our stakeout spot is a bus stop bench about a hundred feet from Promotion Pawn, and it's getting cold. I'm already blowing on my hands every few minutes, and they're currently shoved into my pockets and *still* burning. Why didn't I bring my mittens!? Rookie mistake.

Cedar has already blown his entire allowance on snacks from the convenience store across the street. He's well into his second bag of chips, and we already split a two-liter soda. I'm going to need to pee. Soon.

Things are getting desperate.

"Who do you think it's going to be?" Cedar asks.

"You've asked me that ten times," I remind him, checking my watch again. Still five forty.

"I know. But there are so many options. Didn't you say you knew a thief?"

"Klieba? I don't know. . . . I suppose he did steal some shoelaces. . . ."

Truthfully, I hadn't thought of Klieba. He did claim to be a thief. Had he set me up? Even though he had broken our unspoken vow of silence, it was hard to imagine he'd gone *that* far. And as far as I knew, he'd never even spoken to Coach. Of course, he did steal Mr. Consoli's shoelace for fun. . . .

I make a mental note to add him to the list.

"To be honest, I'm a little disappointed," Cedar says through another mouthful of chips. "I kind of thought this was more an act of vengeance or—"

"Look!" I gasp, pointing down the street. "It's *him*."

Cedar follows my gaze and laughs. "Carl Freburg. I should have known. Notorious troublemaker *and* cut after the first tryout."

Carl walks quickly down the sidewalk, a very full backpack slung over his left shoulder. He looks around nervously and then hurries inside Promotion Pawn.

Cedar sighs. "And here I am with no cell phone. How are we going to take pictures?"

"We'll just have to confront him," I say. "Well—"

"*I* will have to confront him," Cedar mutters. "Yeah, yeah. Let's go."

We take off down the street, with Cedar rolling up his chip bag as we go. I try not to make a scene as a general life strategy, but I know we must look ridiculous charging down the street. Cedar is laughing as we run.

"I can't believe it was Carl. Well, I can, but I can't believe we've caught him already. We're the world's greatest detectives! Coach is going to have to put you on the team, Green!"

Ugh. I forgot about that part.

We reach the storefront, nod at each other, and then Cedar swings the door open and marches inside. I follow for moral support even though I very much plan on avoiding this confrontation. Even so, I can't help but sneak a peek as Carl whirls around, his eyes wide.

A pile of items are laid out on the counter, and Fergus is poking through them.

"*Tree!?*" Carl says incredulously. His eyes go to me. "What are you guys doing here?"

He tries to step in front of the pile on the counter, but Cedar crosses the store in an instant, grabbing his arm.

"Carl, you are in so much trouble—" He cuts off. "What is this?"

My heart is beating like crazy, but I follow anyway, glancing around Cedar's shoulder. Carl looks . . . embarrassed? He rubs his forehead, pushing his straight-billed ball cap up in the process. There's still a tag on it. . . . I wonder if he knows.

But I'm quickly distracted, because the pile of stuff is one of the greatest piles of stuff I have ever seen. Mint-condition Lord of the Rings books. Star Wars action figures. A sweet replica of the *Enterprise.* An alarm clock that is shaped like R2-D2.

It's like a nerd treasure chest.

"Bro . . . ?" Cedar says, turning to Carl.

Carl won't meet his eyes. "I . . . it's my brother's?"

"You don't have a brother!" Cedar says.

"All right!" Carl says, throwing his hands up. "They're mine.
I needed some money for a PlayStation."

Cedar looks between him and the counter. "You were a nerd
this whole time?"

"Why do you think I never have people over?" Carl
murmurs.

I am seriously fighting the urge to play with that *Enterprise*
replica. I nudge Cedar.

"But . . . the ring," Cedar says, straightening up. "Fergus said
you had a ring."

Fergus picks up a small gold band. "He does. But somebody
wrote all over it."

He passes it to Cedar, who stares at it in disbelief, then shows
me. It's a ring all right . . . a perfect replica of the One Ring. It
even has the fiery Elvish font.

Without thinking, I laugh. Well, I choke it down halfway
through, so it's more like a weird, racking cough. But still . . . we
found the *One Ring.* It's the highlight of my whole year.

"I have two of them," Carl says, resigned. "Can you please
not tell anyone, Tree? I know Green doesn't talk to anyone but
you, so I guess he's safe."

Cedar sighs and hands the ring to Fergus. "Yeah. Fine. Come
on, Green."

He turns to go, but I tug on his arm and whisper, "How much does he want for the ring?"

"*Out,*" Cedar says, pointing at the door. "We're back to square one. And probably grounded. Again."

We start for home, and despite everything, I can't stop smiling. I look at him, biting my bottom lip.

"What?" he mutters.

"I can't believe *we* were the ringwraiths all along."

Cedar cracks a smile and slings his arm around me. "We're going to get in trouble."

"I know," I say morosely.

"What do we do next? We don't have any leads."

I consider that. "We go with our gut. This theft wasn't about money. It was personal."

"So . . . ," Cedar says, raising an eyebrow.

"So we figure out who had a motive to hurt Coach. We need to find more clues."

Cedar nods. "We're going to find the culprit, Green. I promise."

"I know." We walk for a while, and then I glance at him. "I really do want that ring. . . ."

"I'll let Mom and Dad know before your next birthday."

CHapteR 16

CEDAR

Recess sucks.

I mean, I loved it, like, a week ago, but now it's the worst. It's the last recess of the day, so it's only fifteen minutes . . . but it feels like fifteen hours. I don't have a phone. First and foremost, recess is *phone time*. It's when I catch up and film any content that needs extras.

Now I just shoot the ball around with the guys, and even that sucks, because Mo and I are still weird. We played bump during lunch recess, and he bumped my ball into the parking lot. The next round I bumped his ball over the kindergarten-area fence, and he had to go inside the school and *through* their classroom to get it. It's the most dreaded of all bumps . . . usually reserved for your worst enemies.

Things are getting serious.

Actually, all the guys are acting strange. Carl went bright red when I saw him this morning—he must have been dreading Monday and my first real chance to tell everyone—but I kept my word. And Corrado, Andrew, and Jerome are giving me dirty looks, like, Can you just admit your brother stole the coach's ring so we can stop running ten thousand wind sprints during practice?

The practices on Thursday and Friday last week were brutal. Coach was moody and every missed shot was another excuse to run us ragged. At one point even Brooks was like, "Is it too late to retire?" And that guy *loves* basketball.

We have another practice tonight, and Coach looked even more sour when I passed him in the hallway this morning. It's going to be a doozy.

I know the guys were talking about Green when I came out, because Brooks is really bad at gossiping. He flushed when I walked over and said, "So, pretty cloudy out today, huh?"

We're thirteen. We don't talk about the weather.

I look around. Most of the guys are on their phones, happily scrolling away. Mo is talking to Corrado while he goes through his TikTok feed. And here I am listening to Brooks go over ideas for a new zone defense.

"Have you talked to Coach about this?" I cut in.

Brooks nods eagerly. "Absolutely! But he said he wasn't in the mood to talk about it. He told me to talk to the guys. He said you specifically."

"Of course he did," I mutter, eyeing Mo's phone.

I am itching to ask someone to use their phone to check my social media profiles, but it's a dangerous move. If my password gets saved onto their phone or I don't sign out correctly I am at their mercy for the rest of my life. Or at least until I can change my password again.

Even so . . . Brooks has a phone. And he's pretty harmless.

I chuck up a shot, figuring I'll ask him, but the ball hits the rim at a strange angle and bounces off toward the street. Just my luck. Sighing, I jog after it. We're not technically allowed to go anywhere near the street, but I can't just abandon my ball.

I scoop it up from beside the sidewalk and freeze. There, walking right toward me, is a group of high schoolers. And not just a random group. I spot Abby walking with some muscular guy eating a hot dog, another short blond girl I don't know, and . . . Keesha Adams.

The Keesha Adams.

She's wearing fashionably ripped blue jeans, a baggy yellow hoodie, brand-new Jordans—I want those kicks so badly—and her long black hair is draped over her shoulders in braids and, okay, I am staring. Is my mouth open?

I can't believe this is happening today of all days. I slept in this morning and my hair is not on its A game. Not to mention I am wearing track pants. Would it have killed me to put on some jeans today?

Oh man, she's looking at me. I force a smile.

"Pass the ball," Keesha says, pretending to pivot to get open.

What is happening!? She's so beautiful I might pass out on the spot. And is she serious? Should I actually pass it to her? Should I pretend to guard her? We might *touch*. I mean, that's kind of the long-term goal, but I wasn't ready to face my ultimate/impossible dreams today.

I try to laugh and it sounds strangely pitchy. That is *not* my laugh.

And most importantly, why am I still holding the ball? Pass it to her. Better yet . . . challenge her to take it from you. *Do something. Anything.* But I just . . . stand there.

"Well . . . you're no fun," Keesha mutters as she walks by with the others.

"He's one of my dad's players," Abby says. "Tree. Ugh, watch your shoes, Keesha . . . this place is a mud pit."

I frown. "Tree is more of a nickname. It's Cedar. . . ."

"How's your brother, Tree?" Abby asks. "Green, right? What's with the names, anyway?"

"I don't know," I reply, trying to think of something remotely cool to say. "And . . . good?"

Wow. Perfect.

"Good," she says. "See you, Tree. Oh, by the way . . . congrats on the video!" Abby calls over her shoulder, then turns to the guy. "Give me a bite of that. You already ate half of my fries."

Keesha doesn't even look back, period. No *fun*? She thinks I'm no fun? How is she ever going to fall in love with someone who isn't fun? Why am I still not speaking? I think my brain is broken.

And what was Abby talking about? Congrats for breaking my mom's windshield?!

I wish Mom and Dad had been that supportive.

"Yeah," I say, trying another laugh. Why is it so shrill!? "I mean . . . bye."

This is the worst moment of my life. I need a hole to hide in. Maybe a well-placed comet.

I hurry back to the yard, hearing Abby and the others talking and laughing behind me. Probably *at* me. I can't believe it. I just blew my first-ever conversation with Keesha Adams.

I skip the ball court and plunk down next to Green at the

back of the portable classroom, burying my face in my hands. He's rereading another Hardy Boys book. Green has been doing some serious research lately. He'll probably be wearing a deerstalker hat any day now.

"Green, my life is over," I moan.

"Is this about the phone again?" he asks, not looking up.

"No." I pause. "Though if I had it, I could totally drown my misery with funny videos."

"I have another Hardy Boys book. . . ."

I sigh deeply. "Does it have adorable cat videos?"

"No, but it has a mysterious lighthouse with a dark secret."

"Fine." I take the book and open it up, though I mostly dwell on the fact that the love of my life just told me I wasn't fun. "Green?"

"Yeah?"

"What does it feel like when you talk to strangers? Like . . . that makes you not talk."

He seems to consider that. "I don't know. I just feel warm and sweaty and like whatever I say is going to be stupid. It's like my brain takes a lunch break or something. Why do you ask?"

"Just wondering," I mutter, glancing at him hopefully. "Any idea how to fix it?"

He shrugs. "Don't talk to strangers."

"Right," I say, deflating. "Did you figure anything out from my Coach notes?"

"Not really," Green says, finally lowering the book. "We still have way too many suspects—"

"Cedar," a new voice breaks in.

I look up to find Mo standing over us. He fidgets, tucking his hands into his pockets.

"Yeah?" I say coolly.

He glances at Green, then lowers his voice. "I . . . well, I know about your 'investigation.' That you're trying to find the ring and all." He pauses. "I'm not saying I know who did it, but—"

Green slowly withdraws his bouncy ball from his pocket.

"Why are you here?" I say.

"Well, I thought you should know something. You know how Corrado hangs out with Carl Freburg after school sometimes? I don't know why . . . the kid's a tool. Anyway, I guess Carl wasn't too happy about being cut. Like crazy mad. And he told Corrado he was going to get back at Coach."

I snap my head up, frowning. *What?*

"Yeah. He said Coach gave his spot away to Green and, well, he was going to get revenge on Coach." Mo clears his throat and turns to go. "I just wanted to tell you guys that."

He hurries back to the court, and Green and I exchange a wide-eyed look.

"Carl didn't want to *sell* the ring," Green whispers. "He stole it for revenge."

"But why not sell it anyway?" I say. "He'll get way more money for a diamond ring."

"Maybe it's still too risky. He might suspect that Coach filed a stolen item report with the police. For all we know, that whole amazing nerd stash was just a ploy to throw us off the scent.

Maybe he's going to wait a bit longer and let things cool down before he sells it."

"All while he lets you take the blame," I say, shaking my head as I watch Carl shooting the ball around. "Carl Freburg, you are going down."

CHAPTER 17

GREEN

"Hello, Opa," I murmur, slinking through the doorway before he can—

Too slow . . . he wraps me in a bear hug. Opa is a big man with a round belly and white hair that is always drifting in the wind. Even inside. It's like it's made out of mist or something.

He was born in Germany a long time ago and Mom says he still dresses the same as he did when he was younger. He always wears brown pleated pants and plaid button-down shirts, and he wears a funny hat called a flat cap when he goes out.

He used to go out a lot when Oma was alive. But she died last year, and Mom says he doesn't leave the house much anymore.

"Looking good," Opa says, nodding approval. "How are you? Still only eating cheese sandwiches?"

"Yes."

Cedar shuffles in behind me, looking despondent. The fifteen-minute drive apparently felt "like a thousand hours" without his phone. I tried to tell him about my fun game of pretending Spider-Man is swinging beside the car on the freeway, but he gave me a mean look so I played it by myself like normal.

He's been bummed since he got home from practice today,

actually. He said Coach was "extra testy" for a third straight practice, and that they ran so many laps half the team almost threw up. Apparently the guys were not too happy afterward. . . . Cedar admitted they were still blaming me for the extra punishment.

"What's wrong with you, Cedar?" Opa asks.

Mom comes in last and kisses Opa's cheek. "He's grounded. No phone for a week."

"Ah," Opa says. "So no more Facebook?"

"Only old people use Facebook, Opa," Cedar mutters.

Opa chuckles. "Well, I'm even too old for that one. I did write an email last week."

"Very good, Dad," Mom says. "And you pressed send, right?"

Mom and Dad bought Opa a laptop last year so he could write his memoirs. Apparently, he called Dad last month and told him something was wrong, and when Dad came over Opa had taken the entire laptop apart because he was "looking for the paper."

Dad had to put the whole thing back together.

"Yep," Opa says proudly, then pauses. "I think."

I make my way to the living room, breathing in the house's familiar smells. Without Oma, the smells of slow-cooking goulash or rouladen on the stovetop are gone. I never ate them, of course, but even I can admit the food always smelled good.

But the other smells are still here. I'm not sure if they're Oma and Opa smells, or just old-people smells in general, but it's like wool blankets and dust and a candle that went out an hour ago.

It's also *very* hot in here. I'm a big fan of undershirts, but not at Opa's house.

Cedar and I plop onto the couch. A soccer game is playing, like always, and Cedar watches that while Mom and Opa catch up in the kitchen. Dad usually comes for visits too, but he's working late tonight.

"So what's the plan for tomorrow?" I ask Cedar, lowering my voice.

He glances at me. "With Carl? I figure I'll just confront him at recess."

"What? That's not how you do an investigation. We need to find proof."

"Can't I just ask him?" Cedar says. "You know . . . and punch him if he took it?"

I sigh. "He'll just deny it. *And* he'll know he's a suspect again and be even more careful. I think we need to check his backpack. Possibly his desk."

"All right," Cedar says, plucking a Werther's from Opa's candy dish. Most of the candies are from when Oma was alive, so we always avoid the jujubes for the safety of our teeth. "But do you really think he'd keep the stolen ring on him? Never mind sitting in his desk. It would be hidden in his bedroom."

"Well, we need to start somewhere. We can sneak into the classroom at recess."

Cedar pops the Werther's in his mouth, makes a face, and spits it back into the wrapper. "Why do those things even exist?" He glances at me. "And that could be risky, Green."

"He's our only real suspect. We have to try."

"I guess." Cedar pokes through the candy dish, then sighs and tries a jujube. He bites on it and groans. "It's like a rock," he says, morosely putting it beside the Werther's. "I miss Oma."

"Me too," Opa says, returning from the kitchen with a tea.

Cedar looks mortified, but Opa is smiling as he drops into his ancient recliner and pulls on a lever to shoot the footrest up. "I tried to make an omelet this morning, and I had so many eggshells in there I needed a toothpick."

I fight back a gag. I *despise* eggs. Not only are they covered in white glass, but they are goopy and rubbery and I can't help but imagine a baby chicken in there no matter how many times Mom assures me that's unlikely. Why would anyone take the risk? You can always be sure there are no jagged shards of death in a cheese sandwich.

"You're doing just fine, Dad," my mom says, even as she rubs her finger along a bookshelf and stares disapprovingly at the dust. "We really need to get you a cleaning service—"

"No way," Opa cuts in, waving his finger. "I don't need anyone poking around my things."

We exchange a curt nod. This is one matter that Opa and I totally agree on.

I was always much closer with Oma. She used to take me everywhere: the science center and the zoo and the movie theater every Sunday morning.

I miss her too.

Opa has a harder time understanding me. He likes sports and outside and construction, and that's a pretty solid list of things I don't like. He and Cedar used to be close, but these days Cedar is usually on his phone the whole time he is here. I can see his hands fidgeting at his sides aimlessly.

"How's school going?" Opa asks, turning to us. "Oh, Green, how did the tryouts go—"

Cedar sighs. "Not good. He didn't make the team."

"Well, you tried," Opa says. "That's all that matters. With a little practice—"

"He was doing fine," Cedar cuts in, sounding testy. "He got accused of theft."

I give Cedar a betrayed look. . . . Opa already thinks I'm batty.

Opa seems to ponder that for a moment. "I'm confused."

"The coach thinks Green stole his late wife's wedding ring," Mom says, who is now dusting the bookshelf. She despises dust. "It's silly, but it's caused a lot of drama. And your foolish grandsons have decided to conduct their own private investigation to find the ring."

"I was just going to recommend that," Opa says, sitting up in his chair. "Can I help?"

"Dad!" Mom says incredulously. "I already forbade them from continuing, thank you."

Opa leans closer. "You know, I was once accused of stealing a toolbox."

"What did you do about it?" Cedar asks with interest.

"First, I punched the guy in the nose," Opa says. "But then I found out another fellow named Franz had taken it, and I punched *him* in the nose. And then I got fired."

Mom rubs her forehead. "That's because the first guy you punched was your boss."

"Nonetheless," Opa says, waving a hand in dismissal. "Less

punching, more finding is the right approach. Let me think. I have magnifying glasses. Binoculars. A fingerprint kit—"

"Cool!" Cedar says, shooting me an excited look. "Also . . . why?"

"Someone had stolen *my* toolbox earlier that year," he says, shaking his head.

"What kind of a job site was this?" I whisper.

Mom storms over, waving her feather duster around. "No one is fingerprinting anything. How would that possibly help? Also, do not listen to your grandfather. He was clearly a menace."

"Still am," he agrees, chuckling and leaning back in his chair again. "I do have a Taser—"

"Sweet!" Cedar says. "And again . . . why?"

"There was this one welder, Fredrick Muller, who—"

My mom points the feather duster at Opa. "Do not give my sons weapons."

"Fine." Opa waits until she goes back to dusting, and then leans in again, tapping his nose. "If you need any backup, let me know. I can be a getaway driver. Or the pyrotechnician."

Cedar is quiet for a moment. "Opa, I legitimately never thought I'd say this, but can you please explain?"

Opa beams and launches into stories about his younger days. And though I learn that Opa has been involved in a shocking amount of intrigue and is possibly also a wanted felon, it's one of my favorite visits since Oma passed away. Cedar laughs the whole time. Even Mom bites back a smile.

Cedar always says you need more people in your life than just family. I disagree.

• • •

"Well, this is a problem," Cedar whispers.

We duck back around the corner and out of view. Carl Freburg is in eighth grade like Cedar, but they don't have any classes together. Carl is in English class during first recess, and the English teacher, the possibly-Coach-hating Ms. Sanders, is sitting at her desk.

We hoped she would get yard duty or at the very least go get a coffee or something. Instead she's grading papers and has a mini kettle and teabags on her desk. Genius. Why risk having to talk to other teachers in the staff room when you can create your own café?

Cedar says Ms. Sanders is very nice, but I doubt she'll let us walk in and search through Carl Freburg's backpack. We did successfully note what his bag looked like this morning. . . . It's pretty standard, but he does have a couple of NHL stickers on the back.

"We'll have to try again another day," I say, looking around the hallway nervously.

I can hear the laughs and shouts from the yard, but there are still a few students walking around who must have gotten into trouble or something. Like we will if Principal Nickel finds us inside. Coach gave us permission for an investigation, but I don't think it was a legal warrant.

I feel anxiety bubbling up in my stomach. I've already got the bouncy ball rolling around my sweaty palm. I'm just not cut out for sleuthing. I really wish Veronica Mars was here. With Spider-Man. What a team that would be.

"No," Cedar says. "I want to get this search over with. We need to get you on the team so we can start practicing again. I *know* it's in Carl Freburg's bag, Green. I can feel it from here."

"You really are like a ringwraith," I whisper. "Also, I really don't want to play on the team anymore—"

"I have a plan," Cedar cuts in. "Ms. Sanders is the AV specialist . . . she's always the one setting things up before assemblies. And guess what? Mrs. Clark needs a PowerPoint cart."

"What for?"

"What—no." Cedar rubs his forehead. "I'm just going to say that and then tell her I had the days mixed up or something. I'll figure it out. Just hide until I get Ms. Sanders out of there."

I turn to him, wide-eyed. "You want *me* to check the backpack?"

"Well, I can't do both jobs!"

Someone clears their throat and we both yelp and turn around. Maggie is standing behind us, wearing some blue coveralls splattered with paint and grease.

She crouches down, grinning. "Staking out a classroom?"

Cedar glances at me, then nods. "We have a main suspect. But his bag is in there."

"I see." Maggie straightens. "I'll clear Ms. Sanders out. But be quick about it."

"You're going to help us raid a classroom?" Cedar says, sounding awed.

She snorts. "*Raid* is a strong word. But yes. Coach is unbearable these days, and he was already a bit much. He spilled some coffee in the staff room today and yelled at the pot. But don't get caught. I can't save you from Mr. Nickel."

I think of getting called into the principal's office and shiver. Only the worst offenders wind up in that office. Some never come out again. You know, without a suspension.

"What are you going to do?" I whisper, risking a glance up at her.

"Simple," she says, heading for the classroom. "I'll tell her I want to confirm nothing is missing from the AV supply closet."

Cedar grins at me. "Told you it was a good plan."

We duck around the corner, and a few moments later I hear two sets of footsteps trailing down the hallway.

"Why would anything be missing?" Ms. Sanders asks, sounding genuinely puzzled.

"You can never be too sure these days," Maggie says. "There are thieves about."

Cedar shoots me a lopsided grin. "Come on."

We scurry into the classroom. My heart is pumping so fast I can hear it in my ears, and I feel a sudden urge to throw up my breakfast sandwich. And by that I obviously mean the cheese sandwich I had for breakfast.

Ugh. Can you imagine if I had *eggs*?

"Find his desk . . . quick!" Cedar says.

In my class we put our bags on a hook by the door, but it appears Ms. Sanders is running the Wild West of classrooms because her students get to take them right to their desks. We split up, hurrying along the rows, and I spot Carl's bag right in the front.

"Here!" I hiss.

"Cover me," Cedar says, hurrying over.

"I think that's more of a war thing—"

"Just keep an eye out!"

Cedar starts rifling through the bag, and I creep back to the doorway, listening for footsteps. We should have come up with a signal for Maggie. She could have made a bird call.

I roll the smooth rubber ball around my palm, mentally urging Cedar to hurry up. Teachers are going to be coming back from the staff room soon. What if Mrs. Strachan catches me in here? Or Coach?

They'll think I've launched a crime spree. There will be an inquisition.

"Where did you hide it?" Cedar mumbles, opening every pocket. "I know you took it." He drops the bag and searches the desk, gagging when he pulls out a rotten banana. *Why?*

"Cedar!" I whisper.

"Just a second. " He sticks his head against the opening, gasps, and pulls something else out. "He has a fidget spinner here! Those were banned. I never did get the craze, to be honest—"

I hear a familiar voice getting louder in the distance. Ms. Sanders.

"Well of course I'm sure!" she is saying. "There are only three carts and they're all there."

"Cedar!" I say, shoving the bouncy ball back in my pocket. "C'mon!"

He starts toward me, throws the fidget spinner back in the desk, and runs for the door. We hurry out together, ready to make a desperate break for the yard . . . and run right into Ms. Sanders.

"Really?" Maggie mouths from a step behind her.

"Why are you boys in my classroom?" Ms. Sanders asks.

She's probably staring daggers at us, but my eyes are locked on my feet. I'm so nervous I am fighting back vomit at this point.

What would Spider-Man do? Well, he would probably be upside down on the ceiling. . . .

"We were on the way to the office," Cedar says. "Green wasn't feeling good."

There is a long pause. "And you fell into my classroom on the way or . . . ?"

My fingers close on the bouncy ball. Of course.

I pull it out and show it to Ms. Sanders. "Sorry," I murmur.

"I kind of threw it to him," Cedar says quickly, sounding convincingly remorseful. "I was trying to cheer him up. He gets down, especially these days with all the false accusations and everything. But I missed him and it bounced in your classroom and—"

Ms. Sanders sighs. "Don't throw the ball in the hallways, boys. Now, if you all don't mind, I have things to do."

The three of us hurry away, and as soon as we're out of earshot, Maggie leans in eagerly.

"Well?" she asks.

"Nothing," Cedar says. "I still think Carl stole it . . . but he hid the ring somewhere else."

Maggie nods thoughtfully. "Well, try to stay out of trouble, boys. I might not be cut out for this after all . . . or at least the distraction part. The problem is I don't like talking to people."

"I totally understand," I say, still feeling a bit breathless from the encounter.

She pats me on the shoulder. "Good luck!"

Outside, Cedar pulls me aside, eyeing Carl suspiciously.

"We're going to have to get him to admit it," he says.

"How?"

"I'll think of something. By the way, genius move with the bouncy ball. You do know what this means, right?"

I nod. "I'm officially a liar."

"You saved us, Green," he says, patting me on the arm. "I'm proud of you."

"I feel like I might pass out."

He laughs and heads for his class. "I'll let you know how it goes with Carl."

"Cedar?" I call after him.

"Yeah?"

"Don't do anything stupid."

He waves a hand in dismissal. "I never do anything stupid!"

"You threw a basketball off a roof!"

Cedar considers that. "I'll do my best."

He hurries away, and I slink toward my usual reading spot, getting a dark look from Allison Gaisson on the way. I'm surprised she doesn't pelt me with a tomato.

Klieba suddenly appears beside me, looking around.

"Check it out," he whispers, pulling a pink paper clip half-way out of his pocket. "I lifted it from Mrs. Strachan's desk this morning."

I turn away, rubbing the bridge of my nose. I *really* hate being a felon.

CHaPteR 18

CEDAR

"Split up into pairs, please," Mr. Consoli says.

I've been dreading this moment. Mo and I have paired up for every class project since the dawn of time. Or at least since second grade. It's not even a question.

We meet eyes for a second. Then I look away. No. Even history can't bring us together.

And I mean literally. This is history class.

Okay. I need to find someone both likeable *and* studious. Also someone who thinks I'm likeable enough to make up for my own occasional lack of studious . . . ness? I glance beside me again, but Mo has already brought his chair over to Corrado's desk. Traitors!

"Hey, Cedar!"

I look up and find a smiling Meghan Hayes looming over my desk. She's holding her chair.

"Got a partner?" she asks.

"Um . . . no."

It's really only half the required question, but she sits down anyway and drops her notebook on my desk. "Perfect! So that video, huh? How come you didn't reply to my DM?"

"I'm grounded," I mutter. "No phone."

Her eyes widen. "I'm so sorry! Terrible timing, too. Are you doing okay?"

Well, at least *somebody* gets the seriousness of this situation.

"Yeah," I say, sighing. "I guess. So, we need to pick out a person for the biography. What about Magic Johnson?"

"Who?"

Oh boy. I try not to look at Mo and Corrado, but I think I hear them high-five and say, "LeBron!"

"I like that shirt on you," Meghan says. "You really know how to rock plaid."

I look down at my plaid button-up. And yeah, the colors are decent, but I'm not sure it's compliment-worthy. For one there's a chocolate pudding stain. I had it for my morning snack.

"Thanks. Anyone you like?" I ask, then feel myself flushing. "Like a . . . famous person?"

She grins. "I know the perfect person: Timothée Chalamet."

"I think he's, like, twenty. Not sure if that's overly historical—"

"Can I ask you something?" Meghan says suddenly, leaning toward me.

Uh-oh. "Okay . . ."

"Is it true? I mean I know *Mo* said it, but it's still kind of hard to believe."

I frown, trying to figure out what she's talking about. I can't help but notice that Keira and Cherene are listening in from the desk next to me as well. Like . . . really intently. "Is what true?"

"That you like Keesha Adams," she says, eyes locked on mine. *"A high school girl."*

She basically spits out the words, and my mouth flops open as I turn to Mo. Another betrayal?! And this one is straight-up evil.

"It was on a group chat," Keira says, leaning in even farther from the other desk. "Is it true?"

A group chat? Mo knows perfectly well I don't have a phone right now. This is low.

Meghan crosses her arms so tightly her elbows are touching. "Well?" she demands.

"Can we just get back to work?" I ask, trying a smile. Save me, dimples!

Meghan laughs in the meanest way possible. "You like her. You're an idiot."

"She is *way* too old for you," Cherene agrees, staring at me like I'm a sad little kid with a crush on Emma Watson. "She's not going to date an eighth grader. There's, like, a rule against that."

"I am aware," I mutter.

"That's why you like all her videos!" Meghan says, looking aghast. "And I saw that heart comment on her last selfie, Cedar. You have been commenting *hearts*. And not even ironically!"

Ugh, I knew those hearts were a mistake. All three girls are laughing at me now.

This has gone too far.

I push my chair back and start for Mo. He jumps as I slap my hands on the desk.

"Well, we are officially mortal enemies," I snap.

Mo at least looks guilty as he glances at the girls. "I didn't mean to—"

"Just hope my finger doesn't slip when I get my phone back. You have secrets too."

Mo's eyes widen. "Bro . . ."

"Don't *bro* me. We are no longer bros."

Corrado holds his hands up, jaw hanging. "Guys, let's not say things we don't mean—"

"Fine," Mo snaps. "You can just hang out with your thieving little brother."

We lock eyes. Mo looks ready to kick the desk toward my crotch. Everyone tenses.

Mrs. Clark glances up from her desk. "Cedar, why are you posturing? Sit down, please."

I give Mo one last glare and return to my desk, heart drumming in my ears.

Meghan glares at me. "Do you know that when you were born, Keesha was already *two*?"

I groan and lay my head on the desk.

When the bell rings for lunch break, I walk out into the yard under a bright midday sun.

I head for the basketball court, where Mo is already waiting. Our whole group is there, in fact, and they all look at one another nervously. They must know a fight is brewing.

"So are we feeling bump or . . . ," Brooks starts.

I snatch the ball from him, eyeing Mo. "How about a scrimmage? Street rules."

Carl Freburg grins and cracks his knuckles. "Sweet. I have some serious pent-up anger."

I turn to him, feeling a fresh surge of annoyance. "I'm sure you do."

We haven't spoken much since our ill-fated pawn shop stakeout, and Carl has been keeping his distance from me. But I've been eyeing him ever since Mo gave me the intel, and I think he's noticed.

He instantly stiffens and balls his fists, as if he's been waiting for me to turn on him.

"What's that supposed to mean?" Carl demands.

"You were pretty upset you were cut, huh? I hear you wanted to get back at Coach."

Carl shifts, eyes flashing toward Corrado. "What are you saying?" he asks quietly.

"I'm saying you told Corrado you wanted to get back at Coach . . . by stealing his ring."

Okay, the last part was an add-on, but Green says good detectives always try to get a reaction. It works. Carl stiffens, his round cheeks going scarlet. He whirls to face Corrado.

"I didn't say that!" he bellows.

Corrado flushes and turns to Mo. "That's not what I told you!"

Mo jabs a finger at me. "I know . . . Cedar is lying!"

"Why did no one tell me anything?" Brooks shouts.

"Give me the ring, Carl," I say, stepping closer to him. "I know you took it."

Carl whirls back to me, his eyes dark. "I didn't touch the ring. Your freak little brother—"

Yeah. That does it. I throw the ball aside and launch myself at Carl Freburg. Again. My anger is aimed at both Mo and Carl, but I *really* don't like Carl.

I punch him hard in the stomach, and he grabs my jacket hockey-style and tries to pull it over my head. We're suddenly all locked arms and desperate attempts to knee each other. He even kicks me in the shin!

Guys are yelling and Brooks is trying to pull me off, shouting, "Can't we settle this over bump, guys?" and then I hear a familiar, booming voice.

"Stop it!"

We both freeze and step apart. Principal Nickel is standing beside us, his bald head looking sweaty from running. He must be on yard duty today.

I'm dead.

Carl points at me. "He attacked me—"

"I *know*," Principal Nickel says coldly. "Cedar, follow me to my office. Brooks, go fetch his backpack. Cedar won't be returning to class today."

With that, he turns to walk inside. The message is clear: I'm getting suspended. And when my mom finds out . . . well. It's all over. She'll kill me. At the very least, I'll never see my phone again, which will totally kill my social life.

I limp after him because that shin kick *really* hurt.

"Cedar?"

I turn and see Green running after me, looking scared. He's clutching his bouncy ball.

"What happened—" Green asks, voice quivering.

"Later," I murmur. "I'll see you at home."

I follow Principal Nickel into the school, leaving a distraught Green standing alone outside.

CHapteR 19

GREEN

I check the clock again. Only twenty minutes until the last bell.

I keep thinking about Cedar. I just want to go home and check on him. We have a work period for art class, but I don't feel like drawing, despite my impressive collection of colored pencils. I have lilac *and* periwinkle. But even periwinkle can't cheer me up.

Instead, I stare at my blank page, worrying about Cedar. It's not helping that everyone in my class is talking about the fight. Most of them are looking at me.

I can hear them whispering.

"I heard he's suspended for a month."

"I don't think that's a thing. Maybe a week."

"Do you think Carl could have taken it?"

"We all know who took it. Even *if* he was mad at Coach, Carl would know better."

I stare out the window, feeling overwhelmed and anxious and like I am going to need to go pee soon. Maybe I really should escape to the Yukon. I could be Gale Bennett, dog-sledder and arctic adventurer. All I would need is a steady supply of cheese slices, bread, and mayo—

"You must feel pretty guilty, huh?" Klieba asks. "About getting Cedar suspended."

I glance at him, frowning. "What?"

"It's not your fault," he assures me, tapping his chest and nodding. "I get it. Kids like us just naturally cause trouble. And sometimes other people get caught in the crossfire."

"Kids like . . . *us?*"

He nods, checking to make sure no one else is listening. "Rebels. Anarchists."

"We're only eleven years old," I murmur.

"We were born like this, Green. Listen, I've been thinking about something big—"

I feel a flash of anger. It's not a common thing for me . . . but when it pops up, it comes on hot. Mom says I used to have a lot of meltdowns when I was little. All the way until the last year or so, actually.

I'm not quite at meltdown level, but I'm getting really sick of everyone assuming I'm a thief.

"I didn't take it!" I snap at him.

Klieba sits back, flushing and looking around. "I know you have to play it cool—"

"Stop it!" I say. "I didn't steal anything. Leave me alone!"

Klieba is bright red now. His mouth is moving but not saying anything. He turns away.

Behind me, Allison laughs and leans closer. "That's what guilty people always say, Green. I watch *NCIS* with my mom every night. Sometimes they get freaks like you on there and—"

"Shut up!"

Okay, I shouted that one. It was almost Coach-worthy. The class goes dead quiet. Mrs. Strachan jerks her head up so quickly she is probably at risk of whiplash. I feel my cheeks burning and my heart is in my ears again and I *really* have to pee.

I grab my bag and run.

"Green—" Mrs. Strachan says.

I ignore her. I sprint down the hallway, feeling tears spill down my cheeks. Mrs. Strachan is shouting after me, but I don't turn back. I know I should go to the office. They'll call my mom to come get me, and I'm guessing she already left work to pick up/yell at Cedar.

But I can't face anyone right now. I burst out the side door and start running.

I don't stop until I am pounding down the pathway through the park, and only then because I run out of air. Then I double over, gasping and crying.

I feel like my whole body is seizing up. My throat is full of cotton balls. My fingers are tingling. Fumbling in my pocket, I pull out the rubber ball and bounce it on the concrete, focusing on that, trying to breathe. I count the bounces to distract myself.

Ten. Twenty. Thirty. How many can I make?

"Green?"

I look up and see Cedar jogging toward me. I'm on two hundred and nine.

He's breathing hard . . . he must have run all the way from home.

"School called to tell us you ran away. . . . Mom's driving the streets, but I said you were probably in the park." He snatches the ball mid-bounce. "Are you okay?"

"That was my all-time record," I whisper, and my voice cracks.

Cedar wraps me in a hug. I thought I'd run out of tears, but I sniffle into his jacket.

"What happened?" he asks.

"They . . . they just kept saying I stole the ring and Allison called me a freak and . . . yeah."

He doesn't say anything for a moment. He just squeezes.

"It's going to be okay, Green," he finally says. "We'll get this sorted out and you'll have another chance at the basketball team and everything will be great—"

I wriggle free, scowling. "Why do you keep saying that? It's a *lie*."

"Green—"

"Everything just keeps getting worse. I never should have tried out. *You* wanted me to be there. You said it was going to be great and I was going to make friends and now everything is worse. Everyone is staring at me and calling me names and Klieba wants to plan a big heist—"

"What?"

"You wanted me to be like you," I shout. "And I'm not. And Dr. Shondez is going to find out about all this and I am going to have go on medication and go to a different school and—"

"What are you talking about?" Cedar demands.

"Dr. Shondez is going to find out I ran away! I have my appointment in one week. And I was trying so hard to be normal and now everything is so much worse." I hesitate. "And, well, they're talking about transferring me to a different school. And giving me medications."

Cedar's eyes widen. "What school?"

"It's a private school. Mom and Dad liked that it had smaller classes and—"

"That's ridiculous!" he cuts in. "You are perfectly normal—"

"No, I'm not!"

I storm past him, feeling tears streaming down my face again.

"Green . . . ," Cedar calls after me.

"Leave me alone!"

I start running again, and this time I don't stop until I'm in my bedroom. I slam the door shut and retreat to the fort under my bed.

"Why won't everyone just leave me alone?" I whisper, curling up in the darkness and squeezing the bouncy ball so tightly my fingers hurt.

CHAPTER 20

CEDAR

"Ninety-three . . ."

I toss the bouncy ball toward the ceiling from where I am sprawled out on my bed, watching it stop just short of the stucco and plummet toward me again. I snatch it out of the air.

"Ninety-four . . ."

I always keep a bouncy ball around for Green emergencies . . . it's the quickest way to cheer him up. But it's not often that I'm the reason he's upset. I'm supposed to be the big brother. The best friend. The protector.

Lately I just seem to be making everything worse. And now I find out that Mom and Dad are considering sending him to another school?

Maybe it's to get him away from me.

Normally, I would distract myself with some serious phone time. I would FaceTime Mo, watch cat videos—if I had a cat I would totally make those—or just play NBA 2K for, like, ten hours straight. But that's not an option either, and it won't be for a while.

Mom extended my phone ban for another week as punishment for the suspension. Not only that, but she said the next strike would be a month-long ban. A *month*! I'd never make it.

And even that threat was tame compared to Principal Nickel's warning: one more fight with Carl Freburg and I will be expelled.

Basically, I'm on middle school parole.

I throw the ball up again, my mind wandering back to Green. About the fact that Allison called him a freak, and how everyone still assumes he stole the ring. It's like shy turned into thief turned into *freak* all within a few days. And the fact that so many people think Green "just doesn't understand it's wrong" is the worst part. They don't get how smart he is.

If they would just talk to him . . . I catch the ball again, pausing. Truthfully, I didn't talk to him either. Or at least, I didn't *listen*.

Leaving the ball behind, I knock once on Green's door and then plop onto his bed, sliding back to lean against the wall and let my feet hang out over the mattress. I can hear Green shifting around in his fort beneath me, probably trying to catch a glimpse of the intruder.

"You can't just sit on top of a fort," Green's disembodied voice mumbles. "It's an act of war."

"Too late," I reply, pretending to yawn. "Maybe I'll lie down."

"Do you know how unsanitary it is to share pillows? People drool, Cedar."

"Oh, I know. Sometimes I wake up and my pillow is *soaked*—"

Green's head pops out, blond hair disheveled, giving me a pretty decent death stare. "Get out."

I raise my arms. "I come in peace."

He scowls and crawls out from under the bed, partially wrapped in his navy blue emergency blanket and not wearing any socks. Wow . . . he really was going to sleep down there.

"What do you want?" Green says, standing warily by the door.

"I came to apologize. For a couple of things. But mostly for forcing you to try out."

Green seems to consider this for a moment, and then sits down beside me.

Our feet dangle off the edge next to each other, and I realize his are already almost as big as mine. Sometimes I forget he is only two years younger than me. I always think of him as my baby brother, and, well, I guess I treat him like one too.

All of those fights with Mom about "babying Green," and I've been doing the exact same thing.

"You didn't force me," Green says finally.

Sunlight is pouring through his open curtains, and Green is blinking and rubbing his eyes—he's been hiding under his bed for almost two hours now.

"I did pressure you a little—" I say.

"No," he cuts in, sounding resigned. "I chose to go. I guess . . . maybe a part of me did want to try it out."

I glance at him. "You wanted to try basketball?"

"No . . . being like you." He rolls a bouncy ball around his left palm. "I guess I wanted to see what it was like."

"Lately, it's not great," I admit. "But I just wanted everyone to see the same Green I do. So I talked Coach into putting you through that first cut, and even though it didn't go well—"

"You did *what*?" Green says, creating that angry sandy-blond unibrow again.

Oh man. I was planning on leaving that little tidbit out. Well, too late now.

"I told Coach that you were just really nervous during that first tryout. I said that you were almost as good as me when we played at home."

"You *lied*?" he demands.

"Well . . . sort of. I mean, you really do play better in the driveway."

"It's a very different game," Green says sullenly. "There's much less physical contact." After a moment, he starts rolling the ball around in his palm again. "I was wondering how I made that first cut. I thought maybe I'd played better than I thought. But I really did stink."

"It wasn't just that. . . . He was already thinking about putting you through! I mean you obviously have potential. You might be taller than me in a couple of years."

Green shakes his head. "This talk is not making me feel better."

"The point is, I've made a lot of bad calls lately. And then I came up with finding the ring and . . . well, it's caused even more trouble. I'm sorry."

Green wriggles his exposed toes. "It was kind of fun searching for clues."

"I know Carl Freburg took that ring," I say bitterly. "But we'll never find it now."

"Why?"

"Well for one, I'm suspended for tomorrow. More importantly, I'm also pretty much banned from ever going near Carl again." I let my arms flop to my sides, dejected. "I dropped the ball and forgot everything we talked about. Like . . . don't attack the suspects."

He nods. "The detective community really does frown on that."

"I'm sorry, Green. I don't think we're going to be able to clear your name after all. Apparently I'm a bad brother and an even worse detective."

Green hands me a spare bouncy ball. He has those things hidden everywhere.

Smiling, I take it and roll it around my palm. "Thanks."

"You're a good brother," Green says. "And an even better best friend."

"How about detective—"

"Not so much. Maybe you should stick to basketball."

I sigh. "Fair enough. I'm going to go prepare for my suspension day without my phone. And by that I mean strip down to my boxers and stare at the ceiling in deep self-pity."

"Well, Mom and Dad will be at work," he points out. "You can play PlayStation all day."

"Yeah. You and I can get some serious gaming in, at least."

"I'll be at school," Green says.

I turn to him, surprised. "You're actually going back tomorrow? I kind of figured you'd take a day off too. You know . . . with the whole running-away thing."

"I have to go back," he says firmly.

"Why?"

Green smiles. "Someone has to continue this investigation. Maybe you can't go near Carl Freburg . . . but I can."

CHAPTER 21

GREEN

I walk into the classroom on Thursday morning and sit down, keeping my eyes straight ahead. The room is filled with whispers and stares . . . the prodigal classmate has returned.

Even Mrs. Strachan looks surprised to see me. She manages a faint "Welcome back."

Of course, I've returned for official business. And this time, I've come prepared. I have my map, my suspect chart, a magnifying glass, a notepad, and a whistle, just in case I manage to corner the thief.

I sit down, open up my notebook, and try to ignore everyone . . . especially Allison.

"I'm sorry, Green," a quiet voice says.

I turn to Klieba, frowning. "What?"

Mrs. Strachan is calling out attendance, but he leans in and lowers his voice even more.

"I should never speak about our . . . hobby in public. It's rule number one."

I open my mouth to protest, and then just nod. "That's . . . okay."

As I raise my hand for attendance a moment later, a thought strikes me. I don't like talking to other people, but I do have a job to do. And Klieba might just be able to help me.

"Klieba, have you heard any rumors in the yard? Like someone bragging about a crime?"

It's a long shot, but maybe Carl told someone he stole the ring. Or maybe there is a whole secret thieves' guild like in The Elder Scrolls. If there is, Klieba and Carl are definitely both in it.

Klieba raises his hand for attendance, then seems to ponder my question. "Well, I did hear Maggie yelling the other day from the boy's bathroom. I was headed to the library to return a book. . . ." He pauses. "I stole the wrong one."

"What was she yelling about?" I ask.

"Graffiti," he whispers. "Someone wrote something in there."

"What did it say?"

"I don't know. I was too scared to investigate. But something bad. She was *not* happy."

Mrs. Strachan appears in front of us. "Anything you'd like to share with the class, boys?"

Klieba and I both shake our heads, and Mrs. Strachan gives me a strange look and goes back to the whiteboard. Once, she might have been happy I was talking to a classmate. Now it's just another chapter of my crime spree.

"I would never betray a friend," Klieba whispers, giving me a sharp nod.

I'm not sure what to say to that, so I just turn back to the front. The graffiti is probably unrelated, but I think it's still worth looking into. I eye the clock, counting down the minutes until first recess.

I need to go talk to Maggie.

I knock softly on the open door, easing one eye around the frame. I like Maggie, but approaching an adult is intimidating without Cedar around. It strikes me that I'm forming a whole crew of investigators now: Klieba the thieving master, Opa the driver/possible felon, and Maggie the muscle.

And Cedar and Green, coniferous superteam, hothead tree and butt sandwich—

"Hey, Green!" Maggie says.

I feel my cheeks burning as I step into the room, trying to make eye contact for even a second because Cedar says that's a good way to let people know you like them. Baby steps.

"Hey, Maggie."

She turns away from an inventory checklist to peer at me. "Everything okay?"

For a second, I feel my breath catch. Then my hand slips into my pocket, closing on the rubber ball . . . and it feels like Cedar is beside me.

When I was little and had a meltdown or wouldn't eat, Cedar would bounce a ball to me and I'd feel better. He'd tell me I had to focus or the ball might wind up "three miles down the street" or bounce into a flower vase and get us grounded. "Just watch the ball, Green," he'd always say.

"Um," I say, finding my voice, "I heard there was something in the boy's bathroom yesterday."

"There are lots of unspeakable things in those bathrooms," Maggie replies, glancing at a nearby bucket. "If those floors could talk . . . But I presume you mean the graffiti bandit."

I nod eagerly.

"I thought you might come," she says. "Given the target."

"Coach?"

"Yep," she says, smacking her lips distastefully. "Written in permanent marker, of course. Nothing I haven't seen before, though I was fresh out of nail polish remover. I have to run out after school today."

"So it's still there?" I ask eagerly.

"Yep. And who knows how long it's been there? It's on the inside of the last stall door. . . . I generally don't see that side when I do a quick clean. Crafty little bugger. Of course, I also thought boys only use stalls to pee on the seats and annoy me." She pauses. "No offense."

"None taken," I say, turning to go. "Thanks, Maggie. I need to go see the message."

"I can just tell you what it says—"

But I'm already hurrying down the hallway. I burst into the boy's bathroom and check the last stall, and sure enough, I find a somewhat faded message scrawled in sloppy print across the inside of the door. The letters are big and ugly. I examine them closely.

COACH NELSON SUCKS!

It's not what I hoped for—*I stole Coach's wedding ring and my name is Carl Freburg* would have been nice—but it's still a lead. Someone in Palmerston public school has a vendetta against Coach.

And this time, I know exactly how to find the culprit.

CHAPTER 22

CEDAR

"How is this possible?"

I throw another sweater aside in my parents' closet. I'm vaguely of aware how insane I must look and how carefully I'm going to have to put everything back to ensure I survive long enough to see the end of my grounding, but also *where is my phone!?* I have searched this entire house. I even went into the attic, and I'm still itchy.

That fluffy pink insulation is evil.

Slumping against the wall, I run my hands down my face, dragging my bottom lip with them and making the world's longest *ughhhhhhhhh.*

I thought for sure I'd find it in here. I know my mom is super smart and will have a good hiding spot, but I can't find it anywhere. She must have a secret hatch. Maybe a vault under the floorboards. *Or* she is so smart she brought it to work with her and . . . oh.

"Idiot," I mumble, and slowly start putting the closet back together.

As I fold up the last clothes and head downstairs, I think about Green and feel concern wriggling its way into my stomach.

Is he actually going to take up the investigation alone? Green can't even talk to anyone, never mind search for clues. He's going to be too nervous and then feel guilty when he gets home. I'll have to cheer him up. We can throw around the bouncy ball on the driveway.

He really does like that game for some reason.

I head downstairs to go flop on the couch, when a loud knock makes me jump. Hesitantly, I make my way to the door. I know I'm thirteen and all, but now that I'm alone in the house I can't help but think of home invaders and deranged neighbors. I wish Mom was here.

I peek through the window, then swing the door open in shock. *"Opa?"*

"Hey, pal!" he says, stepping inside with a bulging grocery bag. "How goes the suspension?"

"Boring. What are you doing here?"

He hangs up his wool coat and cap, letting his wispy white hair spill out. "Well, I heard you were stuck at home alone and figured I'd keep you company. Your mom was worried about you too."

"Did she think I was going to search the house for my phone?" I ask wryly.

He laughs. "No, she took it to her clinic. Just thought you might get lonely, I guess."

"I really wish I thought of that before I searched the attic."

He tsks, examining my skin. "Probably all itchy now, huh? Did you take a cold shower?"

"No . . ."

"Do that first. Then come meet me at the kitchen table."

I eye the bag suspiciously. "What's in the bag, Opa?"

He grins and hoists it up to show me. "Albums! I've got some new photos to add. I've meant to do it for well over a year now, and I figured we would do it together. *And* I can tell you about the family tree while we're at it. Did you know your great uncle was an Ackerman?"

"I have no idea what that is."

Opa starts for the kitchen, chuckling. "Then we have a lot to cover, my boy!"

I flip through one of the albums, eyeing the meticulously organized photos. The albums themselves are labeled with topic and years, but they are also broken down on the inside with colored organizers and sticky labels on every plastic slip. The process must have taken hours.

"I'm guessing you didn't do these?" I say, glancing up at Opa.

He's sitting across the table, staring fondly at pictures as he goes through the stack and then passes them to me to find them a proper home. One must have caught his eye, because he doesn't reply.

"Opa?"

He looks up, smiling, and passes me the photo.

"No . . . this is your Oma's work. Even with those digital cameras, she still printed them all out for the albums. She spent countless hours arranging them."

"I can imagine."

The photo is of Oma and Green. He's probably four or five

in the photo, and Oma has her arm wrapped around his shoulders, holding him close. Green didn't smile much at that age—he was a temperamental fellow—but he's smiling in this one.

Oma always had that effect on him.

I check the three albums in front of me and find the right years, then leaf through until I find a category called *Grandsons* which is, like, ninety percent of the album. Oma clearly liked pictures of us. She was also smart enough to leave spaces in each category, so I find an open slip at the end and put it in. Then I write "Oma and Green" on a little sticker and attach it to the plastic.

"Three down," I mutter. "One hundred to go. This is going to take all day."

Opa laughs. "Green never minded. He did a lot of this too."

"He did?"

Opa looks up, surprised. "You don't remember? Green and Oma used to sit at the kitchen table all day organizing albums. I suppose you were in the yard with me. Or playing on your phone when you got older."

"I find it hard to believe Green would do this for fun," I say.

"Green liked to hear the stories. Or maybe he just liked to hear his Oma tell them." Opa sighs and passes over another photo of him and Oma dressed up. "She had a way with words."

"Did she ever talk about Green's . . . stuff?"

"Not really. She always said it didn't matter what labels they gave him. He was just Green. She didn't even want to hear about medication. She always told me she wouldn't change a thing about him. Except maybe sneaking a salad in once in a while."

I consider that as I look at the picture. This was from the fiftieth wedding anniversary they had the year before Oma died. I'm sitting at a table by myself in the background . . . staring down at my phone. That was the first year I got it. I don't think I looked up from the phone that day.

"She was very proud of you boys," Opa says softly.

"If only she could see us now," I mutter, finding the right spot in one of the albums and sliding the photo inside. "I'm suspended. Green is public enemy number one. We're a mess."

He waves a hand. "A little adversity is a good thing, Cedar. It makes us stronger."

"I just hope Green's okay," I murmur, taking another photo.

"He'll be fine! He's related to me, after all. When I came over from Europe, we were crammed into a smelly ship without windows for three months. Can you imagine the seasickness? And *I* was thrown in the brig. I impersonated an officer to get some pork chops."

"Opa . . . you have serious issues."

"Do you want to hear the story or not?"

Grinning, I put the photo aside and lean back. "Were they honey-glazed or what?"

CHAPTER 23

GREEN

"I'm in."

I glance nervously around the yard. "I haven't even told you what we're doing yet."

Klieba and I are standing by the first portable classroom, just out of sight of Cedar's friends on the basketball court . . . including Carl Freburg. I asked Klieba to meet me here at recess. He technically just followed me over here, but close enough.

It was a bold strategy . . . asking a stranger to help me with the investigation. But I need a lookout, and figure I could do a lot worse than a master thief.

Klieba looks around too, lowering his voice. "It's a mission, right?"

"Yeah . . ."

"Sweet!" he says. "So what are we doing?"

"We're going to borrow a page out of Carl Freburg's notebook."

Klieba frowns. "Like . . . metaphorically?"

"No. Literally. I need to match his handwriting."

"Brilliant," he says, then frowns again. "What for?"

"I'm building a case against him. Are you in or not?"

Klieba glances at a nearby teacher, eyebrows furrowed. "How do we do it?"

"We sneak into the classroom—possibly distracting Ms. Sanders on the way with some sort of AV issue—and then tear a page out. Or maybe a loose test or assignment or something."

He hesitates. "That sounds risky."

"I thought you were a master thief!"

"I am!" he protests. "You saw the paper clip!"

"So you're in?" I ask.

He chews on a fingernail for a moment. "I'm in. When?"

"Right now."

Klieba's eyes widen. "But . . . we didn't do any recon. . . ."

I'm already heading for the school. I'm so anxious that I feel dizzy, but I'm also determined to solve this case. If Carl Freburg wrote the message, he just might have stolen the ring too. Only a true villain would write a message like that. Especially in permanent marker.

Klieba hurries after me. "Do we just walk inside?"

"If we get stopped, we'll say we were sent to the office for fighting."

Wow, I am just full of lies now. Even Klieba is looking at me like I've suddenly turned evil. And . . . have I? In my desperate attempt to prove my innocence, have I become the very criminal I was accused of being?

I have no idea, but the thought is making me have to pee. Not now, bladder!

We hurry inside and slink down the mostly empty hallways.

Well, I'm just walking. Klieba is sticking close to the wall and looking like he's ready to bolt outside at any moment.

I gesture for him to join me at the hallway juncture where we can peer into Ms. Sanders's class, then let out a relieved breath. She's not in there.

"Jackpot," I whisper. "I'll go for his bag. You keep watch."

Klieba grabs my arm. "What do I do if someone comes?"

"Make a bird noise."

"A robin?"

"I was thinking an owl," I whisper. "But any bird is fine."

I notice he is trembling. A lot. And he's not going to have any fingernails left soon.

"Are you okay?" I ask, concerned.

"Yeah. Of course," he says, chewing on a thumbnail now. "Bird noise. Gotcha—"

"Okay, see you soon—" I reply, starting for the classroom.

Klieba grabs my arm again, biting his lip. There is sweat beading on his forehead, and I realize that his hand is shaking.

"I have a confession," he says quietly. "I'm . . . not a thief."

"*What?* What about the paper clip?"

He looks away. "It was my paper clip. I like pink. And I never stole the shoelace, either."

"Why would you lie about that?" I ask incredulously.

Klieba hesitates, still not making eye contact. "Because I wanted to look cool. I thought maybe we would become friends if we had something in common."

"Thieving!?"

He scratches the back of his neck. "Well, I did make a joke

about our unusual names once. You didn't even laugh."

"I'm sensitive about my name," I murmur.

I remember that morning. . . . He made a joke about who had a more unusual name the first day of school, and I completely ignored him. He never said anything to me again until the ring incident came up.

"So . . . you pretended to be a thief so we could become friends?" I ask.

I don't even know what to think about that. I mean, it's ludicrous, but I'm also flattered.

He nods. "And now I'm involved in a heist and I'm freaking out. I've never gotten into trouble before. I feel like I need to throw up. I . . . I understand if you don't want to be friends."

He wants to be *friends*? Somebody wants to be friends with me? Even though I said I didn't need one, it would be kind of nice. I would have a class friend and someone to partner with for work periods and who would maybe stick up for me when Allison Gaisson is mean. . . .

Whoa. I think I do want a friend.

"Well . . . I could use a friend," I say. "You would be my first. Other than Cedar."

"So we can still be friends?" he asks excitedly.

I smile. "Yeah. I'll cross your name off my suspect list as soon as I get home."

"I was on your suspect list?" Klieba asks, sounding hurt.

"Well, I thought you were a master thief."

"Right. Good thinking."

"And don't worry," I assure him, "you can head back outside now. I'll go it alone."

Klieba takes his thumbnail out of his mouth. "I would never leave a friend behind," he says, saluting. "I will hoot at the first sign of danger."

I grin and run into the classroom. Hurrying to Carl's desk, I search his backpack, rifling through a binder. Oh no. Carl uses a computer for his assignments. He's actually extremely organized . . . his binder is *color-coded*. There must be a spare note. An in-class assignment. A—

Then I hear it . . . a shrill *"Hoot!"*

"Balderdash," I whisper, hearing the clack of approaching heels from the hallway.

I look around frantically and slip behind the open classroom door just as Ms. Sanders sweeps inside. She sits down at her desk, and I scrunch up into the corner, my chest tight with panic. I've been caught in the act. Even my bouncy ball won't save me this time.

What's going to happen me? Will I be suspended too? Can two brothers be suspended at once? Will the Bennett family be exiled from town? Will I be grounded? I don't even have a phone . . . what will they take? My bouncy ball? My hour of PlayStation? Oh no . . . what will I do from five to six every day?!

"Hoot! Hoot!" Klieba is shouting outside.

It's too late, Klieba . . . save yourself!

"Who's hooting out there?" Ms. Sanders yells.

"Hoot!"

I can hear Ms. Sanders standing up again. "All students are supposed to be outside—"

"*Hoot!*" Klieba screams at the top of his lungs.

I barely manage to hold back a laugh. Ms. Sanders storms outside, muttering, and I think I can see Klieba sprinting down the hallway.

"*Hoot!*" he bellows on the way.

"Get back here! Who is that?" she demands. "Why are you hooting?"

The sound of heels clacks off into the distance, and I glance toward Carl's bag—no, it's too risky. I scurry down the hallway in the opposite direction of Klieba and Ms. Sanders, figuring I'll go the long way to the yard. Klieba saved my life. Or at least my hour of PlayStation.

He may be my first-ever friend, but he's a good one.

Speaking of which . . .

I stop, looking back down the hallway. I can still hear Ms. Sanders shouting . . . she must be giving chase. My chest hurts and my heart is pounding and I want to run away. But Klieba is in trouble, and I want to be a good friend too.

Taking a deep breath, I shout, "*Hoot!*"

I hear the clack of Ms. Sanders's shoes growing louder as she starts toward me.

Grinning, I sprint the other way and escape into the yard.

"So what now?" Klieba whispers, leaning over from his desk.

It's technically a work period, but it turns out Klieba is really good at math too, so we finished our homework, like, ten minutes ago.

The recess bell went off before we could reunite in the yard, but we both made it back to class unscathed. Well, Klieba told me he had to hide in the boy's bathroom for five minutes, but he said he didn't mind because stress makes him "gassy." Klieba is very honest.

We really do have a lot in common.

"I don't know," I say. "I'm going to need to try again. I just needed a bit more time."

Klieba nods thoughtfully. "Ms. Sanders is going to keep an eye out for burglars. And owls."

"Yeah."

I chew on the tip of my thumb, trying to think. I need a sample of Carl's handwriting. . . . If I can prove he wrote the graffiti and get him in front of Principal Nickel, he might admit to the ring theft too.

"I'll try again at recess tomorrow," I say quietly.

Klieba's eyes dart behind me, and I turn to see Allison leaning forward over her desk, clearly eavesdropping. She flushes and goes back to her work, though she does mutter, "What?"

Allison has been strangely quiet today . . . not a single mean comment. Not even a mention of me running away from school yesterday. It's making me nervous.

Klieba and I exchange a look. This is no place to discuss secret raids.

"So . . . ," Klieba says, straightening up again, "want to come over and play Xbox this weekend? My mom makes awesome pierogies."

I freeze. We've only been friends for *two hours*. I thought I had weeks to prepare myself for a hangout. Maybe months. There are too many unknowns.

How do I politely decline? What would Cedar say in this situation? Probably *Sounds good, bro, I love hanging out and stuff*. Ugh.

"Umm . . . ," I say to buy time. It never works.

"No problem if you don't like pierogies," Klieba says quickly. His cheeks flush a little. "It's a Polish thing . . . never mind. I'm allowed one bag of potato chips a week. Well, a month. But I haven't had anyone over to my house in, well, ever, so this is definitely the time to use it."

I can almost feel Allison's eyes on my back, and I slip my bouncy ball out of my pocket.

"I'm not sure if I can this weekend," I say, trying to think of an excuse. What am I supposed to say? I don't know if I can come over because I don't know your family and what if you are out of toilet paper and what if I need to bounce my ball and—"I have . . . basketball."

"I thought you got cut?" he asks, frowning.

"Cedar and I are still practicing. You know . . . for next year."

Ugh. I'm a full-blown liar now. I'll be a professional con man by the seventh grade.

"Oh," Klieba says, turning back to his math book. His cheeks are crimson now. "Okay."

Great. I've offended my only friend. I try to think. Whenever

I get down, Cedar says something positive. Or he bounces a rubber ball over . . . but that's probably not appropriate here.

I lean closer. "Thanks again for saving me today," I whisper.

That gets a smile out of him. "Any time." Klieba pauses. "Well, not really. I had to stand on a toilet and hold in my burps for five minutes."

I cover my mouth, trying not to laugh. "Fair enough."

"You really think Carl Freburg wrote that message?" Klieba asks. "*And* stole the ring?"

"I don't know," I admit. "But we're going to find out."

CHAPTER 24

CEDAR

"You did *what*?" I ask in disbelief.

Green is sitting on my bed, grinning. He's been grinning since the second he got home from school and bolted up here to tell me about his day. "It was pretty exciting," he says proudly.

"So you actually searched a classroom without me?"

"Well, I had Klieba."

I frown. "The kid in your class who says he's a thief?"

"Yeah, but he's not. Now he's just my friend."

I rub my forehead, trying to process all of this. *"What did I miss today?"*

Green sighs. "A lot . . . but no answers. Klieba and I are going to try again tomorrow."

"I miss one day and my little brother turns into a criminal mastermind," I murmur.

"What did you do all day?" Green asks, looking around my room. "Play PlayStation?"

"Actually, Opa was here. I was adding photos to his albums."

"That sounds fun," Green says.

He's not being sarcastic, and to my surprise, I nod. It *was* fun. Opa told me a bunch more wild stories, and we even took a break to go to his favorite restaurant buffet. We did some serious eating. I put back, like, a hundred chicken balls. Opa said I could join him every Saturday for lunch if I wanted and I was, like . . . uh, *yeah*.

Apparently he's been going alone once a week since Oma died. I didn't even know.

"I hear it used to be your job," I say.

"Yeah."

I glance at him, his socked toes wriggling where they hang out over the mattress. The photos with Oma made me think about something again . . . something I've always wondered about. "Can I ask you a question?"

He looks at me, eyebrows raised. "What?"

"When Oma passed away . . . you never cried. Not when you found out or at the funeral or anything. Why? You guys were so close."

He's quiet for so long I prepare an apology. It was an unnecessary question. I just always wondered about it, since I've literally seen him cry when he was told to eat an apple. Yet he never speaks about Oma. You would think he didn't care . . . but I *know* much he loved Oma.

"Never mind—" I start, but Green cuts me off, still looking deep in thought.

"I guess, for some things, it's too much. Things I really care about. I don't know what to do with the feelings."

I frown. "What do you mean?"

"It's like I get so sad I could just . . . break. So I put it away. I can do that. Turn it off."

"You can turn off being sad?"

I watch as he reaches into his pocket for the ball. "No. That's the wrong way to put it." He rolls the ball around his palm, thinking. "I guess I can just focus on myself when I need to. And if something is too big, I can focus on something small. I can make that more important."

"So . . . you don't think about Oma?"

"I do. But in small pieces. If I thought about it all the time, I would get too sad, and I wouldn't know what to do with all that sadness. Dr. Lee says I'm not good at expressing my emotions. But that doesn't mean I don't have them."

I consider that. "To be honest, I'm pretty good at focusing on myself too."

"Well, we are related."

I smile and climb to my feet. "Want to go play ball? And yes, I mean the bouncy ball."

"Absolutely," Green says, jumping up and following me downstairs. "You excited to go back to school tomorrow?"

"Well, we have another angry-Coach practice *before* school," I say, sighing. I'd gotten an email from Brooks . . . those I could still check on Mom's laptop, at least. "Coach has decided that morning practices will 'toughen us up.' So I get to start my Friday morning with five hundred laps while Coach yells at us for no reason."

I pause, realizing that Green has never had to get ready for school by himself.

"You going to be okay tomorrow? I'll be gone before you even wake up."

Green slips his Crocs on, frowning. "Yeah. Why?"

I bite back a smile and follow him to the driveway. "No reason."

Not that long ago, Green would have been terrified at the mere idea of leaving the house by himself in the morning. Burglars. Fires. Zombies. Now it didn't even faze him.

"First to ten?" Green asks.

"You're on," I say, readying myself.

He chucks the ball straight up the air, and I watch as it spirals toward the asphalt. The ball hits a bump and shoots sideways between us.

We both swipe for it, miss, and then burst out laughing as we chase it across the lawn.

"You call that a screen?" Coach bellows at the top of his lungs. "Five laps!"

Mo groans and shoots me another sour look. It's been the theme of this season's practices so far: I make a bad play, Coach makes the entire team run laps as punishment, everyone blames Green instead of me for some reason, I get upset and mess up again, and so on.

And we have our first game in just over a week. . . . It's going to be a disaster.

We file into an uneven line and start jogging around the gym. I fall in behind everyone else, hoping to avoid the complaints and anti-Green rumblings, but Brooks quickly drops back beside me.

"So you guys never ran like this last year, huh?" he asks, trying to sound casual.

"No" I mutter.

Brooks nods thoughtfully. "And Coach never yelled this much—"

"*No.*"

"Right," he says, wincing.

I feel guilty for snapping at him. Brooks hasn't actually said anything mean about my brother, and I've still mentally lumped him in with the rest of the team. I glance over at him.

"It will get better soon," I assure him.

"I hope so," Brooks says. "We haven't even learned any plays yet. What do we run on defense? What's our inbound play? If we are down by one with a minute left, do we foul or—"

"Faster!" Coach shouts, looking up from his phone. "Pick it up or you get five more!"

Another chorus of groans goes up. I understand cardio is an important part of the game, but this is over the top.

Taking a deep breath, I leave the line and jog over to Coach. He mouths something to himself, brow furrowed, and then starts slowly texting with his thick, unwieldy fingers.

"Hey, Coach."

He looks up, scowling. "Was that five?"

"Not quite," I say, trying to play this as politely as possible. Coach is one wrong word away from an explosion these days. "Everything okay?"

He grunts and keeps texting. "No."

I sneak a peek at the screen and see *Abigail* at the top. It's hard to make out, but I can see a text letting him know she will be late tonight.

And something about Keesha's house this weekend?!

I perk up. "Is Keesha having a party—"

"What do you want, Cedar?" he cuts in, his unblinking eyes shooting up toward me.

"Coach, do you think maybe we're running a *bit* much?" I say, holding my palms up to forestall a tirade. "I love running, personally. It's super. But, well, Brooks doesn't even know what plays we run on offense yet. And we have a game next Friday."

It feels reasonable. I was concise, polite, I have valid reasoning for my—

"Five more laps!" Coach shouts. "This team is soft. We run until I say stop, understand?" He turns to me, only slightly lowering his voice. "Taking your advice hasn't exactly worked out lately. So do me a favor and keep the comments to yourself. Now get going or I'll add twenty more. Got it?"

I feel spit collide with my forehead. Gross. And to be honest, I'm too stunned to move for a moment. That was *intense*, even for Coach.

I open my mouth to say something, close it again, and then hurry off to join the team . . . who are giving me even dirtier looks than before, if that's possible.

"Thanks, Tree," Corrado says, scowling.

Mo just shakes his head.

I fall in at the end of line again, still reeling. Obviously,

Coach has a lot of stuff going on . . . but we aren't going to make it through the season like this. I don't even think I want to.

"Why did you ask him for more laps?" Brooks says, puffing as he runs.

"Dude . . . I didn't ask for more laps."

Brooks wipes his eyes with his T-shirt sleeve . . . his face is drenched with sweat. "Oh . . . good. I was confused. By the way, how does it feel that your video is going semi-viral?"

I whirl on him, almost tripping over my own feet. "What?"

"The windshield video. You have almost a hundred thousand views."

"*What?*"

Brooks looks at me as we run, frowning. "You didn't know?"

"No . . . I've been grounded. And I don't talk to Mo anymore. Why did no one tell me?"

Wait . . . Abby said congrats. That's what she meant! I can't believe this. The one time I don't have a cell phone one of my videos actually gets popular. And it's because I messed it up.

Go figure.

"Want to look at my phone after practice?" Brooks asks.

I'm about to jump at the offer . . . but I know myself. If I see a bunch of messages and comments, I'll feel obliged to answer them all. I have zero self-control.

"No . . . I'll never want to give it back. I better just wait for mine. Thanks, though."

"Start the cycle!" Coach shouts. "Last player sprints to the front and so on. Go!"

A chorus of groans and complaints filters down the team. I

can see the other guys glaring back at me. Even Brooks mutters something.

I sprint for the front of the line, hoping that Green's investigation pays off today.

CHAPTER 25

GREEN

Klieba and I head inside after the morning bell, sticking close to each other among the jostling shoulders. The students are always quieter first thing in the morning, but some of them are basically sleepwalking . . . especially the seventh and eighth graders. It can be hazardous.

"The question is . . . how do we get Ms. Sanders out of her classroom?" I say, trying to think.

Klieba taps his chin. "We could pull the fire alarm? No . . . I think that's an actual crime."

"Definitely a crime."

"What about a mouse?" he suggests excitedly. "We'll let one into the classroom!"

I glance at him, frowning. "Do you have a mouse?"

"No," he says. "But I've heard there are some in the walls. Of course, we'd have to catch one first. . . . Do you have any cheese?"

"Always."

We head for our desks, and I notice Allison is already sitting at hers. She doesn't even look up. She really has been quiet lately. I settle in to my desk, pull out my English book, and—

I freeze.

There's a sheet of paper tucked into my desk. I never leave papers in my desk. Glancing at Mrs. Strachan, I pull it out and almost gasp. It's a pop quiz. And it's *Carl Freburg's*.

I spin to Klieba, showing him the quiz. "Did you steal this?"

"No . . . I thought we were trying again today."

Then who? Maggie? It was possible. . . . She could have "borrowed" the quiz from Ms. Sanders's desk yesterday after school. But why didn't she just match the handwriting herself?

That was a puzzle for later. . . . For now, I finally have my clue.

My hand shoots into the air.

"Yes, Green?" Mrs. Strachan says, looking up from her desk.

"Can I go to be the bathroom?"

She frowns. "You've been here for about fifteen seconds. But fine."

I shoot Klieba a grin and race down the hall toward the bathroom, desperately hoping that Maggie hasn't had a chance to clean the message off yet. I burst inside, throw the last stall open, and . . . bingo. *COACH NELSON SUCKS!* is still scrawled across the door in black permanent marker.

I hold the pop quiz up beside it, comparing the writing.

"Got you," I whisper.

"Well?" I ask eagerly, poking my head into Maggie's office during first break.

Things moved quickly after I brought her the stolen pop quiz this morning. She told me it wasn't her who took it, but she did immediately bring it to the bathroom to compare the writing herself. Maggie agreed it was a perfect match, then she said she would "take it from here."

Then she headed straight for Principal Nickel's office, and the announcement soon followed: "Carl Freburg . . . please come to the office."

"He admitted it," Maggie says. "He said he's regretted it ever since."

"So he did steal the ring," I breathe. "I knew it."

Maggie frowns. "No, no. Just the graffiti. Apparently that was his grand act of revenge."

"But . . . what?" I say, confused.

"Principal Nickel asked him about the ring. He was crying at that point. . . . I felt kind of bad, to be honest, until I remembered I had to buy nail polish remover last night in my off time."

I feel the disappointment welling up inside me. "So he denied it?"

"He didn't do it," Maggie says flatly, shaking her head. "I was there. He wasn't lying."

"You're sure?"

She nods. "He was a mess by that point. He's not the thief."

I lean against the doorframe, crestfallen. "So my only real suspect is innocent."

"Well, *innocent* is a strong word. He has detention for the next five recesses. Of course, we're not even allowed to make students clean anymore. I could have had him mopping."

Now that I think about it, it makes sense. Why would Carl steal the ring *and* write the message? A whole coordinated campaign of revenge? The ring would have been enough, and to be honest, planning that perfectly timed burglary seemed beyond the capabilities of Carl Freburg.

"Thanks anyway, Maggie," I murmur.

She gives me a tight-lipped smile. "Sorry, Green. It looks like the thief is going to get away with it. But hey . . . you still solved a mystery all by yourself. You're really coming out of your shell lately."

"I did make a friend," I say, smiling.

"Then it was a successful day," she says. "See you around."

I wave goodbye and head outside for recess. I guess Maggie's right . . . I did make a friend, solve a mystery, and kind of arrest a criminal. But I still need to find the ring. I need to clear my name, help Cedar get back to normal, and make Coach less shouty.

But who else has a motive?

I head into the yard, looking around for Klieba. Instead, my eyes fall on Allison Gaisson. She's sitting alone with her back pressed against the brick wall like usual, playing with her cell phone. She looks up the second I walk out . . . almost like she's waiting for me.

I hurry past her, then stop, remembering something. Allison was eavesdropping yesterday.

I turn back, eyes wide. "*You* put that pop quiz in my desk?"

She goes beet red and keeps her eyes on the screen. "Maybe," she mutters.

"How? When?"

I don't talk to Allison Gaisson—it's always been a wise life strategy—but this is too much to wrap my head around. One superbully helping me catch another? She was the meanest person out of everyone about the ring theft. And now she's helping me?

Allison shifts uncomfortably, still not looking up. "I overheard you two dweebs talking about it yesterday. And . . . well, I knew I could probably get something. Carl Freburg is on my bus. He's a blabbermouth, and he spends half the time jumping around to different seats and getting yelled at by the driver. So I just sat behind him yesterday and looked through his backpack when he got up. Sure enough, he had a pop quiz all neatly folded in the front pocket."

"But . . . *why*?" I ask.

She doesn't answer for so long that I presume she's just ignoring me, so I turn to go.

"I felt bad," she says finally. "When I said the . . . freak thing. And you ran away from school and stuff. It got me thinking about how everyone turned on you because you're, you know, different or whatever." She lets the phone flop into her lap and looks up. "I don't know. I guess I don't really think you took it anymore. So. Yeah."

"But you've always been mean to me—"

"Because you're a brainiac," she cuts in, glaring at me. "You're, like, a genius at every subject, and you don't even have to pay attention. And you have a really cool older brother who looks out for you, and I don't even have any siblings, and my mom's never home to help me with my homework. But until this year, it was always like: 'Green is special, let's give him special rules and a teacher's assistant, even though Allison Gaisson is *failing* right behind him and no one is helping her!'"

She is full-on shouting now. Her hands are clenched into fists at her sides. And I'm speechless. I mean, I'm generally speechless by choice, but I really wasn't expecting *that*.

I can see a couple of people glancing over. Klieba is by the portable classroom, looking alarmed.

"So you were mean because you thought I was . . . special?" I ask, confused.

She sighs. "I was jealous of you, Green."

I try to make my mouth work. *Jealous?* I'm Green Bennett. The professional Butt Sandwich. I'm so spacey my family doctor wants me to go to a different school and take medications to help me focus. I literally have to go see a specialist *tomorrow* to decide my fate.

"What?" I manage.

Allison shifts. "It's true. But . . . well . . . I realized you have to deal with a lot of stuff too. And I guess I just wanted to help you clear your name. I don't know. Stop bothering me, dweeb."

I don't really know what to do. She isn't making eye contact, and neither am I, obviously, so we both just stare at the concrete. She squeezes her phone. I squeeze my bouncy ball.

I wish Cedar was here. He would know what to say. But it's just me, so I do my best.

"Thank you," I whisper. "For helping."

Allison looks up in surprise. "No problem," she says gruffly. "Was it Carl?"

"He was the graffiti bandit . . . but not the ring thief. I need to keep looking."

She nods. "Well, I hope you crack the case, Green."

I nod and hurry off to join Klieba. My mind is reeling. I've spent an awful lot of time over the last two years wondering why Allison Gaisson is always so mean to me. And in all that time, I never once considered she might be jealous.

If I had that motivation wrong, maybe I'm way off on the ring, too. I just assumed the thief either wanted money or revenge. But maybe the motive was something more . . . unexpected.

I need to get back to my notes.

CHapteR 26

CEDAR

"Dude . . . I can't keep up with you. Now you've assembled a whole team of superthieves?"

Green smiles at me from across the kitchen table. "Sort of."

"I can't leave you alone anymore. Next you're going to be running for student council president." I laugh and shake my head. "I can't believe she bullied you for being awesome."

"That's not really what she said—"

I wave him off. "That's what I heard. Well, I'm proud of you, bro. You're a bigger man than me. Metaphorically, of course. Still, I punch my enemies, and you make peace with yours. Also, we looked at these notes a thousand times, bro. There's no secret answer hidden in code."

Green's endless investigation notes are scattered across the kitchen table. Mom is out doing errands and Dad is bungling around the roof still trying to fix the rain gutter I broke—he's not happy about it—so we figured we could take advantage of the free kitchen.

There are a lot more notes than I thought. Clearly, Green has been working on this alone . . . there are idea webs and detailed "suspect profiles" and also a picture of a ringwraith.

I hold that one up, rolling my eyes.

"We haven't officially ruled it out," Green says. "Let's go over the cuts again."

My theory is still that one of the other boys cut after the first tryout came back. We couldn't officially rule out Mrs. Frost, but honestly, I doubt our vice principal stole a ring. Besides, we have muddy footprints and a bike, and it just seems like they're all connected.

I take out a sheet of paper and write the names of the guys who were cut after the first tryout: *Lee Brownridge, Peter Cotter . . .*

As I'm writing, Green scans through the other papers. He scoops up one of the very few sections I wrote: the first interview with Coach. Seeing it, I feel a pang of worry. We have our first game in less than a week against the dreaded Ormiston Owls, and I've barely gotten any practice in.

"So tell me more about this new friend of yours," I say. "Klieba the master thief."

Green brightens. "Well, he's not actually a thief."

"Yeah, I got that part."

"He likes Minecraft *and* he has a Switch. He even invited me over to play video games this weekend."

I glance up at him, surprised. "And what did you say?"

"Well, I told him I had to think about it," Green says. "I don't know his family. What if I got hungry? What if I have to go to the bathroom and they're out of toilet paper?"

I groan and go back to my list. "Green, you'll be fine. Or just invite him over here."

"Is that an option?" he asks, frowning.

"Yes, Green. I've had Mo over a hundred times." I pause. "Not recently, obviously."

"Do I have more friends than you now?" Green asks, scanning the Coach interview.

"Let's not go too far . . . though, maybe. I'm not sure about Corrado."

"What's this?" Green asks abruptly, turning the notebook toward me. "This scribble?"

I lean over and see a name written in the margin with two question marks: *Layne??*

"Oh, yeah," I say. "Coach mentioned that name. I wasn't sure who he was talking about."

"Hmm," Green says, frowning. "Was that his wife's name?"

I try to think back. "No . . . that was Renee. And I hope not, because he said he was going to talk to her about it."

"Zombie wife," Green whispers.

"I'm sure it's someone else," I say, rolling my eyes. "A friend, maybe?"

Green circles the name. "I think you should ask Coach. For all we know Layne is a loan shark."

I rub the bridge of my nose. "Not this again."

"Just ask him."

"Fine," I grumble. "Here are all the guys who got cut after the first tryout. Five of them. Well . . . minus Carl Freburg. I still can't believe it wasn't Carl. He kicked me in the shin!"

Green reads over the list. "Cedar . . . what if we never find the ring?"

"What do you mean?"

"Do you think people will actually forget about this? Or will I be labeled a thief forever?"

I hesitate. "I don't know. You were right. People just *want* to believe it's you. It's crazy. I know the situation looked bad at first . . . but how can they still believe it?"

"Because I'm Green the Butt Sandwich."

I sigh. "I really don't love that nickname."

"They know I'm different. I had a teacher's assistant until last year. I don't talk to anybody. Some people probably even know I have Asperger's syndrome. So it's just easy."

"Easy to what?"

"Easy to blame someone who's different." Green crosses out a name. "Oma told me that."

"When?"

He crosses out another name. "The year before she died. She was already sick, but I used to sit and talk to her a lot. I had an incident with a boy named Stephen Webster. He threw a book at me in the library, and I threw it back. I got in trouble for starting it, even though it was him."

"Why did no one tell me?" I demand.

"They probably thought you would beat him up."

I pause. "Well, yeah, I still want to—"

"His family moved away two years ago. Anyway, he said I started it, and I still didn't really talk to anyone at the time, so they just believed Stephen. He didn't get in any trouble."

"Where did he move—"

"*The point is* Oma told me I'd have to deal with that some-times. That people would always want to blame me for things because I'm different. That's how I knew this was coming."

I lean back, eyeing my little brother across the table. The gangly, skinny little blond kid with a partial mullet and watery blue eyes who spouts of nuggets of wisdom every few hours. I wish I could dive into his head for a little while. I think there are cogs in there I just don't have.

"We're going to show everyone they were wrong about you," I murmur. "Why are you crossing out names, by the way?"

"I'm using the emotion faces."

"What?"

He looks up. "Anyone who was sad when they saw the list . . . I took them off for now. I want to start with the angry or surprised faces. Those are the kids who would want vengeance."

"How do you remember their reactions?"

He looks at me, shrugging, like, How do you not?

"Green," I say, shaking my head, "you really are different sometimes."

"Thank you."

I stick my fist out for props. "Let's go snag this thief."

He very lightly taps my knuckles, and we sit there for a moment, looking at each other.

"Like . . . on Monday," I clarify. "You want to go throw the bouncy ball now?"

"Definitely." Green starts putting the notes away, filing them into his backpack. He stares at the suspect chart as he puts it away. "It still doesn't feel right, does it?"

"What?"

"That a player took it. That was my only problem with the

whole Carl Freburg theory, and it's still bothering me. It just seems like getting cut from the team is a strange reason to steal Coach's wedding ring. It feels a little . . . extreme."

"What are you saying?"

"I don't know. I just can't help but think that no one in the school had a proper motive. I was thinking about this earlier today. Maybe we're looking at the wrong suspects."

He fishes out his rubber ball and one-hops it across the kitchen table.

I snatch it out of the air. "This isn't about ringwraiths again, is it?"

"It's about Coach," Green says quietly. "I don't think he's telling us everything. You said he's been doing way more texting lately, even during practice, and now this Layne person . . . it just feels like something else is going on."

I want to argue . . . but to be honest, I've been thinking the same thing.

"We'll figure it out," I assure him.

I head to the front door and plunk onto the steps to put my sneakers on. As I'm lacing them up, Green slips into his Crocs and waits by the door, tapping his ridiculous rubbery toes.

"Mom says you have your doctor's appointment tomorrow, huh?" I ask casually.

He nods, chewing on his bottom lip.

"You nervous?" I ask.

"Well, I was accused of theft, ran away from school, had to take a mental health day, broke into a classroom twice, tried to join a thieving guild, still require a bouncy ball to relax—"

"So . . ."

Green sighs and heads for the driveway. "So yeah. I'm pretty nervous."

"Are they actually thinking about sending you to a different school?"

"Yeah," he murmurs, not meeting my eyes. "And maybe medications."

"And this Dr. Shondez . . . she decides if that happens?" I ask.

Green shrugs. "She can't order us or anything. But she's the expert, and I think Mom and Dad will listen to her." He chews on his bottom lip. "I just don't know how to act tomorrow, you know? Like should I be really quiet or maybe I should try to act like you and gel my hair or—"

I take him by the shoulders. "Just be you, little bro. You'll be fine."

"You think so?" he asks uncertainly.

"Absolutely."

We head out onto the driveway, but I feel a little worry wriggling around in my stomach as I throw the ball up in the air. What if Mom and Dad make Green change schools? What if I don't get to see him as much anymore? Lately, I feel like we're spending more time together than ever.

I don't want that to change.

The ball hits the asphalt, we chase after it, and I try very hard not to think about his appointment tomorrow.

CHAPTER 27

GREEN

I wonder if Spider-Man goes to the doctor. I'm imagining him swinging along beside our car, of course, though in hindsight he could probably just sit on the roof. Maybe he even sees Dr. Shondez. Spider-Man, we need to talk about your paranoia. . . . Yes, I know you call it your Spidey Sense, but the medical community calls it anxiety.

People just don't understand super orders. Spider-Man has his webs. I have my bouncy balls. We're both happy.

"What are you thinking about?" Mom asks.

My mom is in the driver's seat, and Dad is sitting beside her. It's Friday morning—she could only get an appointment at nine a.m., so I get to miss a half day and go to school at lunch. I can tell they're nervous. Dad keeps telling me we need to "trust Dr. Shondez's advice." But I don't think they want me to go on medication, and I don't know if they really want to split me up from Cedar, either. But with everything going on lately, they think I'm going to fail this check-up.

And they're probably right.

"Spider-Man," I reply.

Dad chuckles. "Well, just answer honestly today. Okay?"

"Okay."

"I . . . told her a few things," Mom says. "We had a phone call a few days ago to prep."

I lay my head against the glass. Spider-Man does a flip. "You told her about the ring?"

"I told her pretty much everything. I had to. She needs to know about current stresses."

I see the enormous hospital looming in the distance—apparently Dr. Shondez has a clinic next to it.

"Why did you guys name me Green?" I ask suddenly.

"I told you . . . we liked the color," Dad says, glancing back at me.

"But didn't you think it was weird?"

"Well, we knew it was unusual . . . ," Mom says hesitantly.

"Would you still have given me the name if you knew?"

Mom glances at me in the rearview mirror, frowning. "Knew what?"

"That I would have Asperger's syndrome. That I would already be weird. And maybe you should name me Steve or something."

She's watching the road again, so I only get a profile view. Dad seems to be waiting for her to answer, because he looks at her too.

I never practiced the profile views as much, but this is Mom. And I can see her eyes tighten. The words form on her lips. She's thought about it. Probably not about Cedar. It doesn't matter what his name is, because he'd make it cool. But they gave a weird kid a weird name. Green Asperger Bennett.

"I would have still named you Green," she says finally.

"Absolutely," Dad agrees.

I raise my eyebrows. "Really?"

"It's you. You're just . . . Green. And I wouldn't want to change anything about you."

We pull into the parking lot. The clinic rises in front of us . . . a gray concrete slab with narrow windows and other patients heading in and out.

"Are you sure?" I murmur.

Mom parks the car and turns to me, squeezing my hand. "Come on."

"It's nice to finally meet you, Green."

I look up. Dr. Shondez is sitting behind her desk, smiling at me in wide-rimmed silver glasses. She asked Mom and Dad to wait in the lobby so she could talk to me alone first, and now I'm sitting in the office by myself, nervously squeezing my rubber ball in my hand. This appointment is thirty minutes on a Friday morning, but I know it can make a big difference.

I manage a nod.

"I've heard a lot about you, of course. I have a pretty good handle on your medical history, but I'm more interested in how you are doing *now*. So, how are things going lately?"

"Okay," I reply.

I don't meet her eyes. I think it's the white coat. It makes me think about sickness.

"I heard about the missing ring," Dr. Shondez says, writing something down. She has a file open. . . . Mom said Dr. Lee had forwarded everything to her office. It's not, like, bulging, but it's got a fair number of papers in there.

I nod again.

Dr. Shondez taps her pen on the file, studying me. "How did it make you feel?"

"What?"

"Being accused of something like that. I heard the other kids have been hard on you."

I roll the rubber ball around in my left palm. Dr. Lee usually says something about that, but Dr. Shondez doesn't seem to mind. I take my time to respond, but she doesn't say anything. Dr. Shondez seems to be very good with silence.

"It . . . it made me feel bad," I say. "But not all the kids were mean. I made a friend."

Her pen pauses on the folder. "You did?"

"His name is Klieba. We both thought the other one was a criminal. But it worked out. We've talked about hanging out sometime. Probably at my house. It's a logistics thing."

Dr. Shondez seems to think about that for a moment. "I'm happy to hear that. And I was interested to hear you tried out for the basketball team, too. There are notes in here that you didn't want to even be *near* other kids a few years ago. And here you are trying out for sports teams."

"Well, the tryouts did lead to the whole missing ring incident," I point out.

"Why did you try out for the team, Green?" she asks.

I think about that for a moment. "I thought I would try something new, I guess. And I didn't really enjoy it . . . even before the ring. But it was a chance to hang out with Cedar more. I like hanging out with my brother, I guess. . . ." I pause, surprised. "To be honest, I don't really regret trying out. I mean, I didn't make it or anything, but I tried something. I just . . . went for it."

Dr. Shondez smiles. "Can I ask you something, Green?"

"Sure."

"Are you happy? Do you like yourself?"

I frowned. Dr. Lee never asked me anything like that.

"Well . . . yeah," I say.

"Excellent." Dr. Shondez closes the folder. "Then we're all set."

"That's it?" I ask, confused.

"Your grades are good, Green," Dr. Shondez says. "Your mom and dad say you're much more easygoing at home these days, despite all of this school drama. She did mention you still won't eat any vegetables. . . ."

I make a face. Did Mom really think I was going to start with zucchini?

"But I'm not terribly worried about that. What I care about is your happiness and well-being. If you ever want help academically or socially or you start feeling differently about yourself, then I am always available to discuss ways to help. But if you are happy with how everything is going, then there's no need to make any changes right now." Dr. Shondez leans back, tapping her pen again. "Green . . . you're kicking butt."

I laugh without thinking. I guess I never expected a doctor to say *butt*.

Dr. Shondez stands up and calls my parents back in. After

she explains the same thing she told me, Mom leans into me, squeezing my hand. Dad gives my shoulder a shake. It's strange—I'm having my best doctor visit ever when I'm still considered a deranged felon at school. I really don't understand people sometimes.

"And I hope you find that ring," Dr. Shondez says. "From what I hear, you and Cedar have been teaming up on some sort of investigation? That's pretty cool."

I glance at Mom, who looks slightly less happy but still just smiles and rolls her eyes.

"Dr. Shondez . . . can I ask *you* something?" I say.

"Certainly."

"Why did they name it Asperger? I mean, I know about the guy . . . but still. *Asperger?*"

Dr. Shondez bites her lip. "I have no idea," she says, sounding like she might laugh.

"Do you think it can be changed? Can you call a conference or something?"

"Actually, it's already being replaced."

I frown. "It is?"

"Yes." She leans back. "It turns out Hans Asperger was working with Nazi Germany during World War II. He even sent children for experiments. As that revelation has come to light, the scientific community has begun moving away from the name. In the U.S., for example, the diagnosis is already no longer used, due partly to the advocacy of people in the autism community. I think Canada will likely follow suit. For now, most specialists consider it an autism spectrum disorder.

But perhaps we'll settle on something else. Any ideas for a replacement?"

Hmm. I should have been prepared for that. There's *Grunyans*, of course . . . it has historical context. *Wunderkinds* has a pretty nice ring to it, if they decide *Grunyans* sounds too much like *gremlins*.

But now that I think about, neither of those sound right either.

"No," I say, tucking my bouncy ball away. "Maybe no name at all? Just . . . kids?"

Dr. Shondez is quiet for a moment. "I think a formal name can sometimes be a good thing. It helps children realize they're not alone. But you're right. Kids should always be seen for who they are as individuals first."

I look up at Dr. Shondez in surprise, forgetting my eye contact rule. I wasn't expecting her to agree with me.

She smiles. "You know what I see in you? Honesty, intelligence, focus, and a big heart. You just save that heart for the people closest to you."

When we leave, Mom's eyes are glassy.

CHAPTER 28

CEDAR

"You know . . . I only agreed to one interview," Coach grumbles, swiping through his text messages. Or maybe he's using Instagram. *Do teachers use social media?* There's no way.

"This will be quick," I promise.

It's Monday morning, and I'm finally back to school after my two-day suspension last week. And that also means I'm back to detective duty.

He levels a suspicious look at me. "I thought this 'investigation' was over, anyway."

"Because of the fight?"

"Yes," he says in exasperation. "Despite everything, I'd still prefer that my star player not be expelled from school."

"I only get expelled if I attack Carl Freburg."

Coach puts his phone aside and waves for me to continue. "Fine. Hurry up."

Before the screen goes black, I spot an open text message on his phone. It's probably rude, but I've been spying on people's phones lately by instinct. Maybe it's jealousy that they have one, or maybe it's paranoia about another Cedar-loves-Keesha-Adams group chat.

Regardless, even though it's too fast to read the full message I get a good look at the name and the first few lines. And . . . well, that's convenient.

I open my notebook and jot down a few lines, then scan Green's questions.

Green predicted it was probably our last chance to get Coach's cooperation, *if* he even agreed this time, and Green wanted to cover as many bases as possible. I then came along with a red pen and knocked out all the ones related to zombies or Mafia connections. We trimmed it down to three. And at least one of them is suddenly relevant.

I look up at Coach to launch into my first question, then pause. He looks . . . tired. There are dark circles under his eyes and his thinning brown hair is disheveled and a bit greasy-looking.

"Are you okay, Coach?"

Coach flushes and pats down his hair. "I'm fine. Didn't get a lot of sleep."

"Because of the missing ring?"

"Is this an investigation or a therapy session?" he snaps. I squeeze into my chair, taken aback by the outburst, and his face softens. "Abby and I are having some issues lately," he says, glancing at the framed photo. "She's . . . staying out late at night. Just being a teenager, I guess."

"Oh."

"She was fine until a few months ago. Probably has some new boyfriend."

"Did she mention if Keesha has a boyfriend too or—" I say,

and then stop when he glares at me again. "Anyway, Coach, did any of the guys you cut come to ask why or complain? Did any seem really upset?"

"No," he says. "Well . . . Carl Freburg. I heard he wrote me a little note to say thank you."

I nod, writing down *Only Carl Freburg*. "Have you noticed anyone treating you differently lately? Like they seem guilty, or are just straight-up avoiding you?"

"Other than my daughter?" Coach asks dryly. "No. Well, Maggie seems mad at me."

"That's because you blamed Green—"

He waves a hand in dismissal. "I know what she thinks. But I haven't changed my mind."

"I see," I reply tersely. "Last question: Who is Layne?"

Coach straightens up, his eyes darting to his phone. "Excuse me?"

The text was from a *Layne*. And I caught the first two lines, even upside down: "Are we still on for tonight? I'll be at your house at seven . . ." something something. I think she might have been bringing pad Thai. Whoever she is, she has good taste in takeout.

"You mentioned Layne in our last interview. Who is she?"

Coach is bright red again. That man can really flush. He's like a beefsteak tomato.

"That is none of your business," he says. "We're done. See you at practice."

"Coach, we need to know of any possible suspects—"

"Layne did not steal my ring!" he bellows, slamming his hand down. "And don't go around mentioning that name. I never should have gone along with this ridiculous investigation."

There is some serious spit flying now, so I pack up and head for the door.

I pause. "So she's a friend or—"

"Out!"

I run down the hallway, clutching my notepad beneath my arm.

Green listens attentively over last recess as I describe the interview . . . especially the part where Coach got really spitty again. We're tucked against the back of the portable classroom, and Klieba is keeping watch nearby for some reason. He seems like a nice kid, but he's pretty skittish. He made a hooting noise when a soccer ball got kicked over here. I still don't even know who would be sneaking up on us.

"And you're sure about the text message?" Green asks. "You said it was upside down."

I nod. "I'm sure."

"That's actually pretty impressive."

"Bro, if there's one thing I can do, it's read text messages."

Green snorts. "I wonder why he's getting so upset about this Layne person."

"It's suspicious," I agree. "I almost had to shield my eyes he was so red. He looked . . . guilty."

Now that I say it out loud, it fits. He wasn't just mad. He was flat-out *guilty*.

"Do you have practice tonight?" Green asks.

"Yeah . . . and that should be fun. I sense a whole lot of wind sprints coming my way."

"But you'll be home by five thirty?"

"I presume so," I say. "Where are you going with this?"

"Do you know where Coach lives?"

I frown . . . and then shake my head. "I don't know, bro. That's some next-level spying."

"Do you?" he persists.

"I've got a pretty good idea. He made our bus stop there once on the way to a tournament because he forgot our uniforms in the dryer. I could probably find it on Google Maps again. I think it would be a pretty long walk from our place. If we both had bicycles, maybe, but—"

"Bicycles are a hazard," he finishes.

"You could ride on my handlebars—"

Green visibly shudders. "I've already come up with a better plan. It provides transportation *and* an excuse to be out of the house for a while. Plus some adult supervision."

"What are you talking about?"

Green smiles. "We're going to call our getaway driver."

"Opa?"

"He said he wanted to help," Green points out.

"What are we going to say: Opa, can you drive us to a stakeout?"

"Well . . . yeah . . ."

"Dude!" I protest. "He's ninety!"

"I think he's eighty-four—"

Klieba is looking back at us, holding his finger to his lips. I sigh deeply.

"What would we tell Mom?" I ask, lowering my voice.

"That we're going to hang out with Opa," Green says. "I mean . . . it's true."

I glance at the school, thinking about Coach. If he catches us staking out his house, there's going to be trouble. Maybe expulsion-type trouble. But he really is being weird. Whether or not it involves the missing ring, he's definitely hiding something.

"Okay," I say reluctantly. "We'll go stake out Coach's house."

Green claps his hands together, beaming. "Perfect. I'll call Opa as soon as I get home."

"All right. But don't be surprised when he says no. Even Opa has his limits, Green."

"Is this illegal?" Opa asks, reclining the driver's seat in his old Volkswagen Golf.

Green and I glance at each other. We're parked down the street from Coach's house, which is just out of view. We already drove by and scoped the area out. It's pretty ideal for spying. The neighbor across the street has a huge landscaped yard with shrubs and hedges, so we decided we'd use those for cover instead of risking a parked car right out front. It seemed too obvious, and we don't have tinted windows or those cool spy fedoras.

"I'm not actually sure," I admit, glancing at Opa.

Opa snorts and lowers his flat cap over his eyes. "Well, try not to get arrested. Your mother might kill me before I can bail you out. I'm going to have a snooze. How long do you think this will take?"

I glance at my watch. I don't usually wear one, but I borrowed Opa's for the mission. It's already six forty-five. I think. It's one of those old ones without any numbers and I'm not great with those.

"Not long," I say. "Twenty minutes maybe?"

"Well, I'll be here," Opa replies, already yawning. "It's not my first stakeout."

Green and I look at each other, but I just mouth "Later."

"Boys?" he says, lifting his cap again to peer at us with one hazy blue eye.

"Yeah?" I ask.

"Don't tell your mother I drove you."

I salute. "Deal."

We scurry down the street, and as we approach Coach's house, I gesture for Green to slow down and look casual. With our hands jammed in our pockets, we look perfectly inconspicuous except for Green's bright red Crocs.

I spot the perfect hiding place in the neighbor's yard. With a last check to make sure no one is looking, I plunge into a giant shrub. It doesn't go well. There are a *lot* of scratchy branches in here. I make it, like, halfway and I have leaves in my mouth and possibly bugs and I'm pretty sure my whole butt is still sticking out. I slowly climb out again, sighing.

"Should we just duck behind the hedge?" Green asks, biting back a smile.

"Yeah."

We hurry over to the nearby hedges and try to position ourselves out of sight of both Coach's house across the street and whatever master gardener owns this one, but we are definitely in view of most of the other neighbors. It's quiet out—it's mid-October and chilly—but I'm really hoping this Layne person is on time. Someone is going to spot us sooner or later.

Coach's house is a two-story brick home like ours, with a big garage with one of those doors that has a line of windows in it like Dad wants. He has a home gym in our garage and always says "a little extra light would be nice." Coach's lumbering blue pickup truck takes up half of the driveway.

"I can see why spies usually go with the parked-car scenario," I grumble, dusting leaves and dirt off my jacket. "Did Opa even hesitate when you asked him to come?"

"Yes, but only because he thought a soccer game was on. It's tomorrow."

"Right."

"Dog walker," Green murmurs, pointing down the street, and we both shuffle behind the hedge, crouching down to stay out of view. We really should have dressed better. I have a *yellow* jacket on. We wait there as the elderly lady walks by. Her dog sniffs our way, but keeps walking.

"Do you think this is actually illegal?" Green whispers.

"Probably. By the way, did that doctor say anything about you being a criminal now?"

He told me the appointment went "fine" when he got back on Friday, and that he wasn't changing schools, and then we just started playing PlayStation and I forgot to ask anything else.

Green glances at me, smiling. "Actually, she just said I was kicking butt."

"The doctor said you were *kicking butt?*"

"Her exact words."

"Hmm. Well, I've been saying you're completely normal for ages."

Green seems to consider that, eyeing Coach's driveway. "She didn't say that."

"I thought she said you were getting better?" I ask, surprised.

"No," he says, "she said I was kicking butt. I'll always have autism spectrum disorder."

I frown at him. "But . . . you hate all that mental disorder stuff."

"Mostly the name," Green says, watching as a car appears down the street. "But they're getting rid of that anyway because it turns out Hans Asperger was awful. Though, to be honest, Butt Sandwich is kind of growing on me."

"Why?" I ask in disbelief.

"It just makes me laugh. I kind of like saying it. Butt Sandwich."

I rub the bridge of my nose, exasperated. "You continue to surprise me, little bro. But if we were destined to be Butt Sandwich and Tree, so be it. I need to ponder a new theme song."

"Let me know," he says, smirking. "The point is, I would still like to work on some stuff. But Dr. Shondez said I can take my time. And also that I am awe-inspiring. So."

"Well, that clearly went right to your head," I mutter, following his gaze. "Is that car—"

"Yeah."

The beige car pulls into Coach's driveway, and both of us tuck a little more out of view, peeking through the leaves. The lights turn off, and the driver's door swings open.

"Holy meatballs," I whisper as a familiar figure steps out of the car.

We look at each other. It's Ms. Sanders.

She grabs a bag of takeout food out of the back seat—she really did bring pad Thai—and then heads for the front door. I glance at Green.

"Well, it's not much of a lead," I say, disappointed. "I mean, I didn't see that coming but—"

The front door swings open. It's not Coach . . . it's his daughter, Abby. She opens the door, stands there for a moment, then disappears from view. Ms. Sanders pauses, then slowly heads inside. And that's it. The front door swings shut, and our very brief stakeout is over.

I straighten up, blowing into my cold hands again.

"Well, aside from some juicy gossip—" I say.

Green looks deep in concentration. He's mouthing something to himself: "Angry face?"

"What's wrong?" I ask.

He bolts across the street. It's so sudden I don't even have time to grab at him, and I just tuck out of view again and watch as he runs right up to Coach's house, standing on his tippy toes to peer in the garage. He must be trying to find a way to sneak inside. Green has actually become a full-on criminal. What have I done?

I hurry after him before we both get arrested, but he darts

down the driveway before I can get to him, gesturing for me to run.

"I knew it!" Green shouts as we run. "It was red!"

I have no idea what he's talking about. We sprint around the bend and out of view, and Green doubles over, breathing hard. I grab his shoulder and pull him up, scowling.

"Are you just trying to get us arrested at this point or—" I demand . . . then pause.

Green is smiling. "I know who stole the ring."

Chapter 29

GREEN

I pace in front of Coach's classroom door, rolling the bouncy ball around my palm. I want to listen in, but I'm also so nervous I feel like I need to keep moving. I'm right about my theory. I think. Like ninety-nine percent. Or at least ninety. It all made perfect sense at the time, but now that I'm back at school and angry, yell-y Coach is inside . . . I'm starting to second-guess myself.

I think I really did let Dr. Shondez's compliments go to my head. The clues add up, but that doesn't mean it's right. And if I'm wrong—

"Excuse me?" Coach bellows, his voice echoing down the hallway.

I take a deep breath. We knew he would react . . . unfavorably. Cedar reacted unfavorably too. I had to explain it to him ten times. And he was still so leery that he decided to wait until the end of the day, so that we could quickly run home if Coach started screaming.

There's also no basketball practice on Tuesdays, so Cedar figured this was his best bet to avoid wind sprints.

I can hear Cedar calmly explaining things as I methodically

bounce the ball against the ceramic tiles. I normally wouldn't do this inside the school, but technically it's *after* school and the hallways are pretty empty, so why not. It's helping me relax like always. One, two, three—

"That's not proof!" Coach shouts.

I mouth out the proper reply: "We need you to take a look. . . ."

"How do you even know about that? An educated guess? You took an *educated guess*!?"

We really couldn't admit to the stakeout. It's almost certainly illegal.

Nine, ten, eleven—

"Green?" a concerned voice says.

I look up and see Maggie trundling down the hall with her cart. She's wearing coveralls as usual, and a bucket of water sloshes around every time the cart hops over cracks in the tiles. Maggie stops, frowning, as if finally hearing the very loud conversation going on behind me.

"Everything okay?" she asks.

"I think so."

She nods. "Interviewing Coach again?"

"Presenting a theory."

"You know who stole it?" Maggie asks excitedly. "Who?"

I hesitate. "I prefer not to say until it's proven. I don't want to spread any rumors."

"Good idea. Well . . . fingers crossed you're right." She starts walking, then pauses as Coach yells something again. "Maybe I'll stick around until they're done talking. Just in case."

"Thanks, Maggie," I say.

We stand there in silence for a moment, and a thought strikes me.

"Maggie . . . did you really mop a student?"

She snorts and shakes her head. "I heard that rumor. No. I told him I was going to mop the floor with him. Still got in a bit of trouble, of course. But I guess the story changed with time. Stories do that around here, you know."

"I know," I murmur. "Apparently I took the ring as hostage to use it against Coach."

"I heard that one," she says, nodding. "Well, I don't mind being known as the Mopper."

"You don't?"

"Nah. Keeps everyone in line. Why do you think I keep this bucket around? I don't mop *that* much."

I bite back a laugh . . . and then Coach comes storming out of his classroom, throwing his duffel bag over his shoulder. He gives me a *very* unpleasant stare, then storms down the hall.

Cedar shuffles out after him, taking a deep breath. "That was fun."

"Well?" I ask eagerly.

"He's going to go check." Cedar slings an arm over my shoulder. "I really hope you're right."

"Me too," I whisper.

I put too much mayo on my sandwich. Classic mistake. It's not a total sandwich ruiner, but the balance is definitely thrown off.

It's too sweet, and then the cheese gets mushy . . . never mind the bread. Yeah, it's ruined.

But Mom forbid me from remaking my sandwiches because of "minor ingredient imbalances," so I just eat it anyway. They're all having porcupine balls, which is basically meatballs in rice and tomato sauce. I like the name since the rice sticks to the meatballs like quills, and that's just plain clever, but also they just sound sharp and I won't be eating that. Ever.

"So, you boys were hanging out with Opa last night, huh?" Dad says. "That's a new one."

Cedar almost chokes on a meatball. "We like hanging out with Opa. I'm going to start having lunch with him every Saturday." He glances at me. "You're invited too, but why bother?"

I nod. "Agreed."

"What did you guys do?" Dad asks through another meatball.

Mom is eyeing us from across the table. She seemed suspicious yesterday too.

"Just went for a drive," Cedar says. "P.S. Was Opa in prison at some point or . . . ?"

"No," Mom replies, sighing. "He's just not very good at following rules. It's hereditary." Cedar opens his mouth, and she levels a finger at him. "It skipped me. *You* got a double dose."

I snicker into my sandwich.

"What about Green?" Cedar asks.

She wipes her mouth, turning to me. "I'm beginning to suspect he got a dose as well."

231

"I'm just kicking butt in general," I reply.

"He's never going to let that one go," Cedar mutters, holding up a meatball. "You know, most people have meatballs with spaghetti. It doesn't have to be named after a prickly rodent."

"Your father prefers rice. He incorrectly believes it's healthier."

"Feels healthier," Dad agrees, cleaning his plate off and returning to the Crockpot for seconds. "So, Cedar, you must be getting pumped up for the game this Friday—"

He's interrupted by the doorbell. Mom responds first; she puts her fork down and hurries to the foyer, grumbling about "solicitors during dinnertime." I hear the front door swing open.

"Coach?" she says, sounding shocked.

"Evening," Coach says. "Can I speak to Cedar and Green, please."

Cedar looks at me, wide-eyed. My heart starts racing. This is it. The moment of truth.

"Boys?" my mom calls uncertainly.

We stand up together and shuffle to the front door, standing shoulder-to-shoulder. Coach is standing on the porch, hands jammed into his pockets, his eyes on his feet. And, most importantly, he has a chain around his neck. The diamond wedding ring dangles from the end.

"Whoa," Cedar says, squeezing my forearm.

Coach turns to me. "I need to apologize, Green. To be honest, I don't even know where to start." His fingers wrap around the ring. "It was in Abby's sock drawer. Sitting right there."

Mom looks between Coach and me, clearly confused. "Excuse me?"

Coach was definitely crying earlier . . . his eyes are red and puffy. "My daughter, Abby, stole the ring, Mrs. Bennett. I found it in her room, and then spoke to her when she got home from school. It was exactly like Cedar explained. She admitted to everything and stormed out."

"Why would your *daughter* steal the ring?" Mom asks.

"She was unhappy I was dating Layne," he says, flushing. "Uh . . . Ms. Sanders. I knew she wasn't thrilled about it, but I didn't know she was *that* unhappy. She told me she didn't like me wearing the ring around Layne, because she didn't think I could be 'that sad' if I was . . . well, restarting. She took her mother's death very hard, of course. We both did."

"Oh," Mom says awkwardly. "But . . . why not take it from home?"

"I don't take it off much at home. And if she had taken it from there, she said I would have instantly known *she* took it. But Abby knew I took it off at basketball. . . . I told her myself. She just picked her time well."

"So she let someone else take the blame . . . who happened to be my son," Mom says.

"Yeah." Coach clears his throat. "She's in trouble, too. But it's on me, Mrs. Bennett. We're going to take some family counseling. And I don't think Abby knew how hard of a time Green was getting. I told her I thought he took it, but that was all. I guess she figured there would be lots of suspects if it was stolen at school, but no way to prove who actually did it. Of course, it turned out that everyone blamed Green. I'm just grateful that the boys figured it all out."

"Well, I'm glad you found the ring," Mom says curtly. "But this was a serious issue—"

"How did you boys figure it out?" Dad asks loudly.

He's joined us in the foyer now, though he does have his plate with him.

Cedar and I glance at each other.

"You're the detective," Cedar whispers.

I still can't quite meet Coach's eyes, but I manage to find my voice again.

"It was a few things," I say quietly. "Obviously, it had to be someone who knew the practice schedule, and that Coach always took the ring off. So we thought it was someone cut from the team, but . . . well, our main suspect was innocent. I did find out he was a vandal."

"Excuse me?" Mom says.

"That's a whole other mystery," Cedar chimes in. "Go on, Green."

I shuffle uncomfortably. "We knew someone came into the school, because there were muddy footprints after Maggie had already mopped. And I realized they probably had a key. Maggie said she *never* forgets to lock the side door, and she's not the type of person to forget."

"Why would your daughter have a key to the school?" Dad asks Coach.

"I always leave my key chain at home," Coach mutters. "It's got keys for the classroom and the school."

Dad chuckles. "I forget my work keys all the time. Once I had to get Dale to let me in—"

"Uh . . . Dad?" Cedar says, and Dad clears his throat and nods.

"Well," I continue, rolling the ball around my palm, "we still needed a motive. Coach told Cedar his daughter had been act-ing differently lately. He said she was 'avoiding him.' And when Ms. Sanders showed up at the house, Abby looked *really* angry. I've been tested on a lot of angry faces before, so I know the expression, and it definitely wasn't constipation this time—"

"Wait . . . what?" Coach asks.

"Keep it moving, Green," Cedar mutters under his breath.

I take a deep breath and glance up at Coach. "I looked inside your garage and saw a red bike in there . . . just like the one in the surveillance footage. It was Abby's getaway vehicle."

Coach turns to Cedar, scowling. "You didn't mention you were spying on me."

"Did Opa drive you to Coach's house last night?" Mom demands.

There is an awful lot of staring going on. I know I should deny everything . . . but I can't.

"Yes," I say.

Cedar sighs. "Wow. You even sold out *Opa*."

"I don't want to lie anymore," I murmur, eyes down again. "I never liked that part."

Mom and Coach are both quiet, clearly upset, but Dad just whistles.

"Man, I've been missing out," he says through another porcupine ball.

"We'll discuss the various lies and felonies later," Mom says. "Coach, I'm happy you found your ring. But Abby aside, I'm still upset that *you* falsely accused Green."

"I know," he says quietly. "And I'm sorry. I know it doesn't make amends, but a deal is a deal. Green, I'd like to formally offer you a spot on the basketball team. And to start game one. No one is being cut . . . we're just going to use eleven roster spots. I will also make an announcement to the staff and the team that Green was not responsible, and I'm sure they'll all spread the story from there. I'll make sure everyone knows *I* was wrong."

I'm not feeling particularly excited about the whole basketball thing, but I nod. "Thanks, Coach."

"I, uh, obviously have some things to work on," Coach says. "See you boys tomorrow."

He hurries outside, and Mom closes the door while Cedar and Dad congratulate me.

"You made the team!" Dad says, clapping me on the shoulder.

"Our brand-new starter!" Cedar says. "We have got to start practicing first thing in the—"

"You spied on Coach's house?"

They both fall quiet. Mom is glaring at us, arms folded tightly across her chest.

"You continued the investigation without my permission, involved your poor Opa, broke who knows how many trespassing laws, and then accused Coach's daughter on a *theory*?"

"Well, it was correct—" Dad murmurs, taking another bite.

"I should ground you both!" Mom cuts in, pacing around the living room. "Let's review: We have two fights, an elbow to the jaw, a suspension, a broken windshield, an escape from school, who knows if anyone is even doing their homework anymore, and . . ." She stops, turning to us and sighing. "And you stuck together through it all. To be honest, I've never been prouder."

Cedar and I look at each other, surprised.

"So . . . we're not grounded?" Cedar asks hopefully.

Mom wraps her arms around both of us, squeezing us in for a hug. "Not this time." She releases us and turns to me. "I've been thinking about what Dr. Shondez said for a while now. I owe you an apology. I wasn't giving you the voice you deserve. I'm sorry."

I give her another hug. I'm happy she's going to give me a chance to speak for myself more, but I also know she meant well. "I forgive you."

She smiles. "Thank you. And that was a pretty impressive deduction, Green."

"I couldn't have done it without Cedar," I say. "We're a team."

Cedar claps his hands together. "Yes we are. Speaking of which . . . go change into your shorts, Green. We have a lot of practicing to do!"

With that, he bolts up the stairs. I follow him, feeling a fresh knot of worry. I'm really glad Coach found his ring. I can go back to not being a felon, Coach can stop yelling at pigeons, and everyone will be happy. Well, maybe not Abby. Though she wasn't happy anyway, so this is probably better. Maybe not Opa either. I totally sold him out.

But other than that, things are looking pretty positive. Cedar and I are basically the new Hardy Boys, and we officially solved the Case of the Missing Ring.

And, as a reward, I now have to start a fiddle-sticking basketball game. In front of a crowd, in three days.

Super.

CHAPTER 30

CEDAR

I can hear the other players jostling and shouting through their drills on the far side of the court, while Coach does his best not to yell because he said he was "working on his temper." He spoke to the entire team before practice today, explaining that Green did nothing wrong. Green and I stood to the side while he spoke, and a few of the guys at least had the decency to look guilty.

Mo was stone-faced. Not a single word.

Coach decided that Green and I could have a one-on-one practice today. It's risky, since we only have one more practice after this before the big game, but I wanted to work on some of Green's fundamentals. And I also wanted to avoid any more . . . incidents.

We could have just gone home to practice on our own hoop, but Green needs to get used to the gym. He gets spacey in fluorescent light.

"Now watch," I say, getting onto the post with my back to the rim. "You get the ball down here, and you back up as far as you can. Use your butt to keep the defender off of you—"

"There's an awful lot of butt-checking in this sport," Green mumbles.

He looks like the noob to end all noobs today. I was so distracted with training that I forget to monitor what clothes he chose. . . . His shorts only make it halfway down his thighs, he's wearing a T-shirt with a cartoon dinosaur on it, and while he did manage white socks, they're pulled up his shins. If Green was wearing glasses, they would definitely be taped in the middle.

"Just watch," I say. "Step back, pivot, and . . . easy layup. The crowd goes wild."

Green scratches the back of his neck. "How many people usually watch these games?"

"Not many," I admit. "It's the home opener, so we might get a few more than usual. It's after school, though, so not many. Maybe, like . . . fifteen?"

He pales. *"Fifteen?"*

"Dude, the pros play in front of twenty thousand. Now you try."

Green takes the ball and turns his back to the basket, sticking his bony limbs in all directions like a disoriented chicken. He puts his hand up. "Pass me the basketball . . . dude."

I sigh deeply. "Just 'ball' is fine." I throw him the ball. "Now post up."

Green catches the ball, sticks his butt out, spins, and . . . lays it up.

Whoa. That was decent.

"Dude!" I shout, running over for a high-five.

It's a light one, of course. Apparently if we miss a high-five we are at "serious risk of overextending our fingers." Green has a never-ending list of possible injuries.

I can't believe it's actually happening. Green is on the team. He is going to start an *actual game.* Despite everything, my master plan worked. By tomorrow, everyone is going to know Green was innocent. And he already made one friend . . . what's to stop him from making more?

He's going to be a star player and it's going to be like, Let's invite Cedar and Green to all our birthday parties, they're both so cool. I can see it now.

"All right," I say, scooping the ball up. "Let's talk about free throws. . . ."

"Hey."

I glance back and see Mo standing behind us, fidgeting. The rest of the team is on a water break, and Coach seems to be watching the exchange nervously.

"Hey," I say, instinctively stepping closer to Green.

"I'm sorry, Green. I never should have blamed you. We're . . . happy you're on the team."

I want to say something. Actually, I want to say a bunch of things. Like, Of course you shouldn't have blamed him. Or, I told you he was innocent and you're supposed to be my best friend, bro! Or maybe, Want to hang out later? He is my best friend. But I just wait for Green.

"It's okay," Green says quietly. "You did give us a lead."

Mo glances at me. "And sorry I didn't believe you, man. I'm a tool."

"Missed you, bro," I say.

We pull each other into a half hug, clapping each other on the back at the same time. I think we hold it for a second too long because we both shake it off after and try to play it cool.

"Can I come see the cats this weekend?" I ask gruffly.

"For sure, bro. They've missed you." Mo sticks his fist out to Green for props. "And from now on, I got your back too, Green," he says. Green gently taps his knuckles, and Mo laughs and tries again. "Dude, you got to hit that fist hard—"

"We don't need any bone bruises before the big game," I cut in.

Mo raises a bushy eyebrow, then just shrugs and starts back for the team. "So, do you ever get your phone back?" he calls over his shoulder.

I hold back a sigh. It's been eight days. And they really have felt *long*. "Soon, bro!"

"Now that you've gone viral, we've got to come up with some sweet new trick shots."

"How many views am I at?" I call after him.

"Two hundred thousand! This could be it, Tree! We just need more windshields!"

I laugh and turn back to Green, who looks anxious again. I lower my voice.

"Still nervous around Mo?" I ask.

"No," he says. "Just thinking about the game. I don't really want to play, Cedar—"

"If you don't want to, you don't have to," I assure him. "But just imagine it, bro. After all this, you can walk out on that court. You can show everyone how wrong they were. And you and I can play ball together and . . ."

"Make friends and be popular and do trick shot videos," he finishes dryly.

"We'll work up to the trick shots. You can do this, Green."

His face scrunches up for a moment, as if thinking about that. He glances at me, smiles, and nods. "Fine. But if somebody elbows me in the face, I am going to be very upset."

"I will make no promises," I reply. "Now . . . free throws!"

"We're not doing any push-ups today, are we?" he asks suspiciously.

"Well—" I say.

"Cedar!"

We sit around the locker room. Knees bouncing. Fingers twiddling. Nervous glances and deep breaths and Coach pacing around the room with a clipboard and his ring dangling from a chain.

He says he's going to wear it today to remind himself to stay calm. I really hope it works.

Green is sitting beside me, fingers gripping his knees. He's always pale, but he looks whiter than his shin-high socks today. But most importantly, he's wearing a bright blue Palmerston Panthers jersey. We don't get names on the back or anything, but that doesn't matter.

My brother is officially on the basketball team.

He glances at me, chewing on his bottom lip. He looks like he might throw up.

"We're going to be fine," I say. "I promise."

He gives me a look that clearly says, I've heard that before, but he nods.

Coach Nelson clears his throat. "Well, boys . . . game one.

We've had an interesting couple of weeks of practice." He shoots
Green another apologetic look. "But we're all here nonetheless.
I don't expect total perfection tonight. I just want to see hustle,
teamwork, and a no-quit attitude. We lost to the Ormiston
Owls twice last year. Let's send them a message this time."

"What message?" Mo asks. "You want me to trash-talk their
Insta page?"

Coach scowls. "What? No. Just a general message that we're
better this year."

Mo looks down at his phone, fingers poised. "So . . . not on
Insta?"

"Put your phone away!" he bellows, then takes a deep breath,
wrapping his fingers protectively around his ring. It's like Green
with his bouncy ball. "Just . . . have a good game."

I jump up and stick out my hand out. "Panthers on three.
One, two, three . . . *Panthers!*"

The guys run out, but when Green and I go to follow them,
Coach turns to Green.

"Son, I'll be rooting for you out there."

"Thanks," Green mumbles.

Coach looks at me. "And if I get angry, please remind me to
calm down, Cedar."

"Can I say *chill out*?" I ask hopefully.

"I would prefer *calm down*," he says. "Come on."

Green and I jog onto the court, taking our starting positions. I
hear a *lot* of noise. Cheering and applause and foot stomping . . .
way more than usual. I turn toward the bleachers.

"Whoa," I whisper.

There are way more than fifteen people here. Mom, Dad, and Opa are all sitting in the front row, waving and cheering. Opa makes it to a lot of my games, but Mom and Dad must have gotten off work early today. I spot Green's teacher, Mrs. Strachan, and his new friend, Klieba. Even that Allison girl is here.

A lot of other teachers are there too. Ms. Sanders. Mrs. Clark. I spot Maggie leaning against the bleachers in her overalls, who gives me a curt nod. And there are a lot more fans too . . . a lot of younger ones around Green's age. His classmates, I'm guessing.

That makes sense—they all came out to see Green play. Guilt is probably part of it. Most of those students—and some of the teachers—have been treating Green badly for weeks, or at least assumed he was the thief. But maybe they also want to see a happy ending. I know I do.

I glance at Green, who is out on the court with me as a starter. He looks terrified. The Ormiston Owls are waiting on the other side, leering at us in their yellow uniforms.

All that's left now is to play.

"There's a lot of people watching," Green murmurs.

"Yes, there are. It's time for the coniferous superteam to shine. You ready, little bro?"

He shoots me a nervous grin. "I'm ready."

Okay, I'm freaking out. It's the fourth quarter. Less than a minute left. The Owls have the ball and a two-point lead. Coach is shouting instructions way too loudly and drawing up a complicated defensive zone during our last time-out. All of that is pretty normal. Except for one tiny little detail.

Green is still in the game.

He's standing beside me, his jersey clinging to him like Saran Wrap. He's not magically playing amazing or anything, but he's had his moments. He has six points. Three rebounds. He hasn't been targeted constantly on defense. He's spaced out once or twice, but I've managed to snap him out of it. And he's going to be on the court for the final minute of play.

That's right. Green Bennett is a *closer*.

"Then we get the rebound, get up the court, and let Cedar win us the game," Coach says, drawing an arrow to the hoop and a bunch of exclamation points.

"Let's go!" Mo shouts, jumping around and slapping everyone on the back. He gets really amped up at the end of games.

We run back onto the court, waiting for the Owls to inbound the ball.

I glance at Green. "Remember—"

"Stay close to my man," Green says, nodding. "I know."

I laugh and turn back to my own check. "We got this, bro."

If we win this game, the gym is going to go *bananas*. And I am going to win it for us.

The Owls charge up the floor, spreading out on offense. The ball flies around the perimeter, and everyone is shouting and pointing and Coach is trying very hard not to lose it on the sideline. The clock is ticking. If the Owls score, we'll be down by four and in big trouble.

We need to stop them here.

The ball goes to Green's man, who turns and puts up a one-handed floater and . . . it falls short. The ball bounces off the front of the hoop and right into Green's waiting arms.

We're out of time-outs. We need to go.

"Here!" I shout, and Green passes me the ball.

I check the clock. Twenty seconds. We'll have the last shot of the game . . . but I push it hard up the floor anyway. If I have an open layup, I'll take the quick tie and see if we can hold off on defense. But as soon as I get across half court, the Owls converge on me. I'm quickly double-teamed, and even though I try to drive around them, I'm forced into the corner. Their strategy is clear: They're not going to let *me* score.

A double team is a pretty easy trick to get around. The fact that two people are on me means that someone on my team is wide open. I look around and . . . it's Green. I should have known. Green is still the lowest scorer on our team, and the Owls purposefully left him open, daring me to pass it to him.

I check the clock. Four seconds. Well, here goes nothing.

With a quick shot fake, I pass the ball to a wide-open Green.

He catches it. Three seconds. We don't need the clock anymore because every single person in the gym seems to be counting down. I can even hear Maggie shouting. Two.

Green hoists the ball.

One.

He shoots.

Time seems to stop. I watch the ball sail through the air as the final horn sounds, spinning perfectly, thinking that all that shooting practice was so worth it. The ball slowly descends toward the hoop . . .

And hits the back of the rim and bounces away. The Ormiston Owls begin to cheer.

As the Owls run around high-fiving and chest-bumping, my teammates lower their heads. It was a good game. It's just hard to remember that when you lose.

Green is still standing in the same spot, looking from the hoop to the clock, as if surprised that *he* had just taken the last shot of the game. He probably didn't even know it was the fourth quarter. His pale blue eyes follow the celebrating Owls, then fall on me as I walk over to him.

"I guess we lost, huh?" he asks.

I'm usually a bad loser. But today, I just wrap my little brother in a hug.

"Nah," I say. "I don't think so."

Suddenly I feel arms patting my back and realize the whole team has gathered together around us. Green looks at them, bewildered.

"Great game, Green," Mo says, grabbing both his shoulders and shaking him.

"That was so close!" Brooks says. "I can't wait to practice tomorrow. Way to go, Green!"

Green and I meet eyes as more and more of the team congratulates him, and the look of surprise and delight on his face makes everything worth it. I look past him and see the crowd cheering too, and gesture for him to look. Even Allison Gaisson is clapping. Klieba is jumping around, pumping his fist. Mom and Dad are hugging. Opa tips his cap at us. Maggie is beaming.

"What is happening?" Green murmurs. "We lost."

"You won when you showed up today, Green," I tell him. "Let's go celebrate."

"Green, Green, Green!" Mo shouts, and the team takes up the chant.

Green is ushered off the court by the cheering team . . . right past the very confused Owls. I catch a few of them glancing up at the scoreboard, as if to double-check that they actually won.

"Long story," I say as we walk by, then sling my arm over Green's shoulders and join the chant.

CHAPTER 31

GREEN

I don't really have anything against basketball. I mean, it involves bouncing a ball, so technically it's got everything I need in a sport. It's all the other parts that bother me. The yelling. The sweating. One of those Owl kids ran into me, and I swear a droplet of his sweat went *into my mouth*. It was . . . salty. I barely managed to avoid throwing up right in the middle of the court.

Long story short, I quit the team. Coach almost fell off his chair when I told him. The team even tried to get me to change my mind. But I told them that basketball just wasn't for me.

Of course, I'm playing basketball right now. In the driveway. With Cedar.

Just how I like it.

He spins and puts up a shot, wearing a thick sweater and a toque. It's late October now, nearly Halloween, and it's pretty cold. It's already getting dark at, like, six, and I almost fell asleep halfway through my dinner sandwich yesterday.

"You know," Cedar says, passing me the ball, "you could still rejoin the team."

"No thanks. It was cutting into my PlayStation time."

"No it wasn't!" he protests.

"Well, it could have. Not worth the risk."

Cedar rolls his eyes as I sink another layup. "I still don't understand why you even played the one game. It went pretty good, other than the loss. Everything went according to plan!"

"*Your* plan," I remind him. "Remember when you said I could do anything?"

"Yes . . ."

"Well, I wanted to prove that was true. But the point is, I don't *want* to. I like my routines. I like doing the stuff I already do. Though I am hanging out with Klieba tomorrow."

"You're going to his house?" he asks, surprised.

I snort. "Of course not. Not until I can be sure about the snacks and toilet paper."

Cedar just laughs and wrestles the rebound away from me. "Fair enough. Oh . . . Coach took your recommendation, by the way." He sighs. "Carl Freburg is officially back on the team."

I grin. "Good."

When I told Coach I was "retiring," I suggested Carl Freburg take my roster spot. I'm not even sure why. I guess I figured I didn't really know his story either, just like Allison, and I felt guilty that Cedar and I assumed he was the ring thief because he was mean. We caused a lot of trouble for him. Besides, Carl really does deserve to be on the team . . . he's much better than I am.

Coach still wasn't thrilled about the graffiti message—no one likes to be told they suck, I guess—and told me he would "think about it." But I guess he agreed with me after all.

Cedar shakes his head. "I still don't know about that one. He kicked me in the shin, bro."

"You did knee him in the groin," I point out.

He pauses. "True. Well, once again, you're a better man than I am. Except at basketball."

He takes off down the driveway, dribbling between his legs, and hits a three-pointer.

"I'm surprised you're not filming this," I say.

Cedar shrugs. "Maybe later. I'm cutting back on my phone time a little."

"I noticed. Why?"

He scoops up another rebound, lays it up, and turns to me. "I still use it a lot. But . . . I don't know. Maybe you rubbed off on me. I've started talking to Opa way more again, and we do lunches on Saturday now and stuff. And I feel like I talk to Mom and Dad more now too. And, hey, my best friend is already right beside me."

"Mo?" I ask, looking around.

"*You*, dingbat."

"Is your phone charging right now?" I ask suspiciously.

"It's definitely charging," he says. "But that's all still true. I can't just get rid of it, obviously. I mean, I made a viral video. And, much more importantly, Keesha sent me a DM."

"She did?" I ask, stopping mid-shot and turning to him.

I know how much he loves Keesha Adams. He's so weird. She's in high school.

"I almost fainted when I read it," Cedar says. "The message was a week old, dude. I didn't reply to Keesha Adams *for a week*."

"What did it say?"

He grins. "And I quote: 'That video was hilarious. Hope you're not in too much trouble.'"

I wait expectantly, then frown. "That's it?"

"*That's it?!* She wrote me, bro. She hopes I'm not in trouble!" He looks away dreamily. "I wrote her forty-seven replies before I finally settled on one. It was three paragraphs long."

"I don't know much about these things, but that sounds like a lot."

"Yeah, it was terrible," he agrees. "But still . . . we have officially messaged each other."

I laugh and take the shot. "So you're really not mad that I quit the team?"

"Nah. If you're happy, I'm happy," he says, grabbing the ball and tucking it under his arm. "I talked to Mom about this last night. I was trying to fix something that wasn't broken."

"What do you mean?"

"We don't need ball, bro. We're already the perfect team."

I grin and pull the bouncy ball out of my pocket. "A couple throws?"

He laughs and rolls the basketball aside. "Sure. Listen: quick thought. How do you feel about a TikTok detective series? You and me. Maybe Mo cameos."

"No."

"Check it out: We solve mini crimes. One-minute videos. Maybe a theme song—"

"*No,*" I say.

"Butt Sandwich and Tree," he sings, "the coniferous team, they may sound absurd, but they're a sleuthing machine—"

I laugh and throw the ball straight up into the air, and we both watch as it descends toward the bumpy asphalt driveway, waiting to see which direction it will bounce. That's what I love about this game . . . it doesn't really matter.

Wherever it goes, we'll chase after it together.

EPILOGUE

Abby hesitated on the front porch, debating whether or not it was too late to hop back on her bike and take off again.

No one was making her do this. It was clearly the *right* thing to do, but it was also deeply embarrassing. She chewed on a way-too-short fingernail, tasting salt. She really had to stop eating French fries in the cafeteria every day . . . especially since Emerson stole ninety percent of them. She was supposed to go to his house after this, and he'd asked if she would pick up more taquitos.

Sighing, she knocked on the front door.

Cedar answered. His eyes widened, and for some reason, he looked behind her, like she might have brought bodyguards or assassins or something.

Strangely, he looked disappointed that she was alone.

"Hey," Abby said, awkwardly rubbing the back of her neck. "Is your little brother here?"

"Uh . . . yeah." Cedar called upstairs for Green, and soon a slightly shorter, even skinnier version of Cedar appeared. Green's big blue eyes widened too, and then he stared at his feet.

He also reached into his pocket to grab something. Was that a . . . bouncy ball?

She raised an eyebrow. These kids were weird.

"Listen," Abby said, "I just came to say sorry. I probably should have come to your game last week, but to be honest, I am too embarrassed to ever set foot inside that school again."

She tried to catch Green's eyes, even crouching down a little, but he refused to look up. He must have been really angry with her . . . and she couldn't blame him.

"I know I caused a lot of trouble. Especially for you, Green. So . . . yeah. I'm really sorry."

"It's okay," Green murmured. "I know why you did it."

"Well, it didn't really make much sense," Abby said, digging her foot into the porch. "I was trying to punish my dad. . . . I guess I just wasn't ready to move on. To be honest, it felt wrong the whole time, but I didn't know how to fix it. I really was angry. I know I should have just talked to him, but I thought I would teach him a lesson." She glanced at Green. "I was happy when you two figured it out. My dad and I got to talk and just put everything on the table. You guys did me a favor."

"Well, we try," Cedar said, grinning.

Abby smirked. "You two should start a detective agency or something."

The two brothers exchanged a grin.

"Butt Sandwich and Tree," Cedar whispered.

Abby frowned. Yeah . . . they were *really* weird. "You guys are pretty close, huh?"

"Best friends," Cedar said proudly.

Abby thought about that. It was nice to see a family acting like that. It was something she missed. "Well, if I hear of any more big mysteries popping up, I'll know who to call," she said.

She tried one last time in vain to catch Green's eye, then turned to go.

"Abby?" Cedar said.

"Yeah?" she said, glancing back.

He hesitated. "Would you put in a good word for me with Keesha?"

Abby looked at him for a moment, and then burst out laughing. "That's who you were looking for! You have a crush on Keesha?"

"Maybe," Cedar said, his cheeks flushing crimson.

"She's in high school, dude. You have no chance. Tell you what . . . we'll talk next year."

Cedar sighed. "Fair enough. I hope everything works out with your dad."

"Me too," she said, thinking of when she'd left . . . the disappointment in his face that she was taking off for another evening. "See you later . . . Butt Sandwich and Tree. I don't get the butt sandwich part, by the way."

"It's for the best," Green whispered.

She hopped onto her bike and saw the two brothers high-five as she pedaled away. She smiled. Family was complicated, of course, but at the end of the day, you only got one of them.

Abby rode for home instead, deciding to spend the evening with her dad.

AUTHOR'S NOTE

This story of two brothers is, in fact, based on three.

When my little brother was first diagnosed with Asperger's syndrome, there was confusion in my household. My older brother and I had no idea what it was, besides the fact that I thought it was pronounced *assburger* for several years, and that it was supposed to explain our brother's behavior somehow. If you read this book, you're familiar with some of his routines:

- He really did just eat cheese sandwiches.
- He was distant and reserved with everyone but family.
- He made friends reluctantly, if at all.
- He was (and is) brilliant.
- He was (and is) hilarious.

I wrote this story to celebrate all those points, and more. He became Green, while my older brother and I merged into Cedar for simplicity's sake. This story is fiction, but the heart of it reflects our dynamic growing up: a younger brother who marched to the beat of his own drum, and the protective older brother(s) who quickly learned that he was marching along just fine.

The history of Asperger's syndrome is both fascinating and complicated . . . and the name itself is rightly on its way out. Not only did Asperger's become part of an umbrella diagnosis of autism spectrum disorder (ASD) in 2013, but the revelations about Hans Asperger's ties to the Nazi party have led to further calls to move past the name. However, many individuals still consider themselves as having Asperger's syndrome, and the term is still prevalent today. The diagnosis can also vary by country. This story takes place in Canada, where clinicians use the ICD-10, a classification system that includes Asperger's syndrome. As mentioned above, the U.S. switched to the DSM-5 in 2013, due in no small part to the advocacy of people in the autism community, and Asperger's syndrome is no longer diagnosed there.

There are millions of people around the world affected by ASD, many of whom are undiagnosed. This book is not meant to minimize or make light of any of the challenges those individuals have had to face, which can include serious effects to their health and quality of life. It's a personal story about one of the people I know best, and a reminder that the names that matter most are the ones we give ourselves.

The doctors told my mom that my little brother would likely live with them his entire life, struggle to form meaningful relationships, and have difficulty holding a job. Well, he's getting married to the love of his life, owns a home, has a job, and, as Dr. Shondez put it, is flat-out kicking butt.

And if he wasn't doing all those things, well, I would have written this book anyway.

Why? Because, like Green, my little brother is awesome.

We have a lot of neurodivergent individuals in my family,

and I share these stories with readers because I want them to know they're not alone. Green didn't need any help when he saw Dr. Shondez, but the option was there, and it's *always* a good idea to ask for help if you need it.

If you ever feel alone, please remember to speak about how you're feeling with loved ones, seek out professional assistance, or access online resources like www.nimh.nih.gov.

My little brother had the first read of this book. He loved it. In fact, he and my older brother are my first readers of every book, and they are my most trusted sources of feedback.

Butt Sandwich and Tree(s) are still going strong.